BANSHEE CRY

RAVEN HUDGINS

Also by Raven Hudgins

Death Callers
Death Callers
Banshee Cry

To all the dreamers, keep your heads high in the clouds

Acknowledgements

I want to thank all of the people in my life who have helped me to achieve my goal. I personally want to thank my husband for always being there and never giving up on me despite being a Debby-Downer at times. Thank you to his family and mine for always believing.

Chapter 1

Not all stories have a happy ending: mine sure didn't. I wasn't giving up, though. I would find a way to bring Kaelin back, no matter the cost.

~ ~ ~

Training day—the once a day grueling task of fighting whatever creature Remy, the wizard I'd accidentally set free from the Abyss, could think of at that time. Today it was a goblin. A sickly grey creature that barely came up to my hip, its legs were little stubs, and its teeth were yellow and razor sharp. So far, it was winning.

"Aislin, you need to keep your feet spread and eyes focused on your opponent's face," Remy called, pushing up his glasses.

Right, keep my eyes on something that was half my size. Not only was it small, but it was quick too—despite me landing a couple hits. That advice, however, wasn't helping. Remy was a record playing on repeat. I took a deep breath and let it out. I spread my feet and adjusted my stance, flexed my fingers on my staff and locked eyes with the goblin. It snarled, its jaw hanging awkwardly, showing off a mouthful of daggers. I grimaced. It lunged.

I dodged to the left and circled around. The goblin swiveled to face me and lunged once more. Its teeth grazed my chin. I reared back, stumbling. My grip tightened on my bow staff as I steadied myself. It crouched, beady eyes narrowing, and charged. I tensed and waited until it was inches away before using my staff to flip over it. Rookie move. Nails dug into my wrist as it yanked me down.

My body slammed into the mat. All the air was sucked out of my lungs. Black spots swirled in front of my eyes.

"That's enough!" The goblin vanished in a puff of smoke.

My pulse pounded in my ears. I closed my eyes and laid there for a moment longer. Damn it. I'd lost, again. I pounded my fist on the mat and sat up, opening my eyes. Why couldn't I beat the damn thing? Zero and three. I ran a hand through my hair, fingers snagging on the hair tie. I pulled it out and my soggy hair fell onto my bare shoulders. I cringed. Second worst thing about training day. The first was cuts and bruises, along with sore muscles.

I rolled my shoulders, wringing out the tension. The year was almost up. Only two more months until Hell. All the preparations had been made. All that was left was for me to be ready to face anything that came my way. The problem: I was far from ready. We weren't even sure what I'd find down there, anyways. How could I prepare for the unknown?

Still, I had two months left. I pushed myself to my feet. It didn't matter. Either way I was going to find him and bring him back. Kaelin, the love of my life. His death was on my hands. His blood had coated my clothes. I gulped, my stomach summersaulting. Bile filled my mouth. I pressed a hand to my belly, where a dull throb ached. A blade through my gut. Almost a year later and the pain remained.

"Let's take a break." Remy handed me a towel.

I took it gratefully and dried my face. Tiny red dots and smears speckled the white towel. I winced. Blood was so hard to get out. I hung it around my neck and let it soak up the rest of my sweat. I sighed and allowed my body to sag. Every muscle hurt. Every inch of my skin felt like pulverized meat. I shuffled to the corner of the room, where my makeshift bed and duffle bag were.

BO wafted in the air. Clothes yet to be washed were crumpled and stuffed inside. I wrinkled my nose as my hands rummaged around for what I was looking for. My fingers wrapped around my plastic water bottle. I unscrewed it quickly and guzzled as much as I could before I had to take a breath. Water drippled down my chin.

"You sure you want to do this, Aislin?"

I turned and faced Remy, wiping water droplets onto the back of my hand. Was he being serious? After everything I'd been through, he thought I wouldn't do it?

"I'm not losing him again," I said between clenched teeth. Heat rippled across my skin.

Remy winced, bowing his head. His glasses slid to the bridge of his nose. I sighed, guilt washing over me. It wasn't his fault that we were in this mess to begin with.

"Sorry, it's just . . . I can't give up on him, not without at least trying to get him back." I ran a hand down my face. "I thought, maybe, you would understand that."

Remy's face darkened. "I do," his teeth snapped together, "but remember what happened to me. I don't want you to suffer the same fate."

I shook my head and lowered my gaze. "Too late for that. The Court will come for me sooner or later despite what Illium says. I'd rather go out fighting than to just surrender."

He sighed. "Go wash up. I'll see you in my study in an hour."

I nodded and listened to his footsteps as they faded into the background. The showers were the only place to relax. My feet took over. Down the hall and to the left. The rest of my body was unresponsive. Ten months we'd been in this studio. Ten months of training non-stop, with a side project here and there for cash. Remy sold potions and elixirs on the side. For what, though? I'd never be as ready as Remy wanted. No amount of training could ever truly prepare me for what was to come.

I let out a breath, my shoulders sagging. The studio was just that, a studio—for dancing I assumed. There were two main rooms: the study and training room. The only other room was the showers/bathroom area. Cobwebs and dust clung to the highest corners. A crack ran down the middle of the ceiling. The place was a mess, but it was better than nothing.

It had been almost a year since I'd lost Kaelin. Sometimes it felt like an eternity and other times like yesterday. My heart clenched. His death still haunted my dreams. The crumpling of his body, his golden eyes turning lifeless—all of it was burned into my mind. I lost my heart and soul that night. Sometimes I thought I could still hear him-the rumble of thunder when he laughed, his teasing voice . . . and then there were times when I thought he was still here, talking to me.

The day I turned eighteen, and had my first Death Call, was the day I lost everything.

In a blink of an eye, I lost not one, but two of my best friends. It still felt surreal that Teagan, one of my closest friends, had made the ultimate sacrifice. To reach a banshee's true form, she had to relive the sorrow of all the people she had lost from her Death Calls and end her life.

She never regretted her actions, though. I closed my eyes, letting the pain of losing them both wash over me. If only she was still here, with her sharp green eyes and motherly attitude. Teagan was the oldest of our group, the one with the hardened heart-or so I had thought. Despite knowing the consequences of loving another, she had done it, again. Aaron paid the ultimate price, but so did she. A single tear trickled down my cheek. I needed to be strong. If I was going to save Kaelin's soul, I needed to harden my heart and let go of regret. Both would only drag me down.

Taking a deep breath, I strode through the shower room. I stripped quickly. The cold air nipped at my exposed skin. I turned the knob for the hot water. Water sputtered and splashed, but it didn't take long to heat up. Steam enveloped me in its warm embrace. I stepped into the spray of hot water and sucked in a breath. The heat stung my open wounds, but the pain quickly subsided. The aches of my muscles dissolved, loosening the tension in my back.

"Wow . . . just beautiful."

I stiffened at the words and spun around, my arms up in a fighting stance. No one was there. The white tile stared back at me. The splashing of water echoed through the room. I shook my head. My imagination was playing tricks on me again.

"What I wouldn't do to touch you right now, Linny."

A sob escaped my lips. I covered my mouth, my hands shaking. That was the nickname Kaelin had given me when we were kids. My eyes searched the showers, heart pounding in my ears. *Please, not this again.* A week after his death, I thought I saw him walking down the street. In my desperation, I'd chased after him.

"Kaelin, stop—it's me, Aislin," I'd called after him. He didn't even turn around, just ran down one of the side roads off the beaten path.

My pulse raced, matching my labored breathing. Only a couple days before, I'd been discharged from the hospital with my stomach stitched up from the damn near fatal sword wound. Running was probably not in my best interest, but I couldn't stop now—not with him a foot or two away.

I'd pushed myself harder. Kaelin swerved to the left and into the woods. I followed close behind. The air around us turned frigid. I shivered. The trees cast a dark shadow on his form from the setting sun. The dark hues made him stand out more. He stopped suddenly and stood still. My heart leapt. I stumbled forward and grabbed his shoulder, turning him to face me. My insides froze.

"Long time no see." Kaelin had grinned, revealing pearly white fangs.

"N-No, it can't be," I'd sobbed, staring into cold eyes. Silver not gold.

The image of Kaelin vanished—in its place stood a vaguely familiar guy. Spiky black hair framed his deathly pale skin. Flashes of my time with the court ran through my mind. I had released him from the Abyss and in return he had tried to eat me. If it hadn't been for Illium's interference, I wouldn't be standing here.

"I'm so glad you remember, sweet thing. Now then," he stepped closer and cupped my cheek, "let's finish what we started. I promise I'll be gentle." He closed his eyes and licked his lips, his nostrils flaring. "Just as sweet as I remember."

I'd been paralyzed—whether it from fear or something else, I wasn't sure. Magic, maybe? His mouth descended, but instead of going for my neck, he'd kissed me. His lips were feather light, and for a moment my body had relaxed on its own accord against him. That was my mistake.

A smile lifted the corners of his mouth then pain ripped through my bottom lip. I yelped and pushed him away. A metallic, coppery taste filled my mouth. I pressed a finger to my lip and pulled it away. Red tinged my finger—my blood. My eyes widened.

Red eyes flashed, inches away from my face. Hands grabbed me. Pain laced up my neck. I struggled, kicking and punching at any open area I could. Words formed in my head. *"You're so beautiful. I shall make you mine. Mm, sweet as honey on the tongue."*

Fear had gripped me. Was this my death? It was fitting though—going out the same way Kaelin had. I relaxed in his arms, pretending he was my love. There was no point in fighting anymore. If this was the end, then I hoped it came swiftly. Inky spots entered my vision before darkness clouded it completely.

"Aislin? Damn it to hell," someone muttered. There had been a shrill scream, then nothing.

I shook my head, water droplets splaying on the tiled wall. It wasn't until later that I found out who had saved me. Remy, once again. From what he'd told me, some vampires had the ability to get into a person's mind and make them see what they wanted to. The voice I'd heard had been the vampire's thoughts, an aftereffect of feeding.

A vampire's mind opens when they feed—something about it having a calming effect on the victim. I wasn't sure if I believed that. The thing was, Remy had killed the vamp, which meant there was either another vampire after me or I was seriously going crazy. The latter seemed more plausible. Chills ran up my arms despite the warmth from the shower.

I closed my eyes and tilted my head back, running fingers through my matted hair. The heat from the water calmed my frayed nerves. Stress, that's all it was. Stress of trying to be prepared—to fight through the pain. Would it ever go away?

"Damn it, Kaelin, you promised you wouldn't leave me." I sighed and leaned further back. The knobs of the shower dug into my spine. I didn't care.

Tears trickled down my cheeks, masked by the collecting water droplets. Hollowness filled me. My hands shook at my sides. I balled them into fists and slammed them back. Pain rattled up my arms. What if I never got him back? Would I be empty forever? Was loving someone else possible? Teagan had done it, but look where that had gotten her.

My childhood friend, Teagan had tried to love again, but wound up losing him too. To Kaydynce, no less. I had saved Kaelin that time at least, but I couldn't save Aaron. No one tells you about the fine print—a Death Call isn't just for the banshee's first love. Loving a banshee is a death sentence. I shook the thought off. There was no way I was losing him. I showered quickly and got dressed.

I knew Remy was waiting in his office for me. Voices or no voices, I had to focus. If not for me, then for Kaelin. I walked out of the shower room and back into the hall. The study was just up ahead on the right. I took a deep breath and entered the spacious study. Remy sat behind a big oak desk with his hands folded in front of him. Bookshelves stood on either side of the room, encasing it. Rows upon rows of books lined the shelves. Half were covered in dust, but there were some that looked brand new. The newer ones were what Remy had purchased himself. A single lamp lit the room to the left. It cast a soft glow on his ebony skin.

I cautiously stepped into his line of sight. Dark brown eyes reflected in his glasses as he lifted his gaze toward me.

"All right, Aislin, we need to discuss a few things. Why don't you have a seat?"

I raised an eyebrow, glancing around at the study. Seat? The only seat in the whole room was the one Remy was sitting in.

"Oh, sorry. Hold on a second." He sat up and lifted his hand, whispering something in Latin.

There was a loud pop then a chair materialized out of thin air. I jumped back. The chair wobbled and fell on its side.

"Wow, I didn't know you could do that, Remy." I studied the chair before righting it.

Remy rubbed the back of his head. Pink tinted his dark skin. I grinned.

"It's just a simple relocation spell, nothing special," he said sheepishly.

I rolled my eyes, taking a seat. "Any sort of spell is special to me, especially since I don't have your kind of talent."

His cheeks darkened. "Thanks, Aislin." He cleared his throat. "Anyways back to business. I think we need to pick up your training, and I mean big time. We only have two more months before embarking on this dangerous mission you are so intent on. Fighting goblins isn't helping, so we need to go bigger."

My eyes narrowed as I frowned. "What do you mean by bigger?"

Remy sighed. "We need to change the environment you're in, make it unpredictable." I crossed my arms over my chest, waiting for him to finish. "What I'm trying to say is, we need to take the battle outside of your comfort zone—like out in the open of the town. You know, where you let loose a bunch of nasty creatures."

"You have got to be kidding me! It's not like I knew what I was setting free. How was I supposed to know that there were a bunch of criminals locked up?"

Remy leaned forward. "From what I was told, Illium told you not all of them were there unjustly. But that is beside the point right now. These creatures have been loose for almost a year now and are wreaking havoc throughout the town."

Ugh, Illium. He was the elf that helped Kaydynce and I save Kaelin from being executed, but also opened the portals to release every creature from the Abyss. A favor for a favor. Well three, technically. Save Kaelin, make sure the Court doesn't come after us, and release everyone from the Abyss. Two of which he'd failed.

I looked away, hands clenching. "Isn't that the court's job? Plus, if I track down and fight these villains, who is to say I won't lose or worse get caught by the court in the process?"

He smiled weakly. "That's a chance we are going to have to take, Aislin. It's now or never—you need to get stronger. My training ability isn't up to par with what you are going to be facing in Hell."

I crumbled into the chair, suddenly feeling drained. The weight of what I was about to do pushed down on me. I ran a hand through my damp hair. He was right though—fighting goblins, fairies, and the like were a piece of cake compared to the demons and other atrocities I'd be facing in Hell.

I sighed. "Fine, I'll do it, but if I die or get captured by the court again, I'm blaming you."

Remy chuckled, pushing up his glasses. "Don't worry. Didn't Illium say the court wouldn't be coming after you? Also, I hardly think he would let you die—you have a favor that needs to be completed for him, if I'm correct."

My shoulders slumped even more. "Thanks for the reminder."

Chapter 2

Aislin

The moon's soft rays glowed on the sidewalk. I shuffled my feet. The feat that Remy had put me up to was ridiculous. The court could be anywhere, and I was essentially out hunting them. Silence filled the streets. I scanned my surroundings. Nothing moved. Houses lined either side of the city street. In the dark, everything looked the same. I ran a hand over my face.

I was definitely out of my comfort zone. Between a row or two of apartments were dark alleys, the perfect place to find Esor Animis—soul eaters, and Nocturna Suppressions— nightmares. Two of the three supernatural clans. I shivered.

Street lamps flickered on either side of me. I wasn't in my home town anymore. From what Remy had said, there had been several killings in the next city over. I gritted my teeth, pulling my jacket tighter against my body.

The air was frigid despite how warm it had been earlier in the day. My bow staff, which was just a stick now, was clutched to my waist. Two nights I had been out here, searching for anything amiss or out of the ordinary.

Two nights, I'd found nothing.

The hairs on the back of my neck stood up. My whole body stilled. This was what I had been waiting for. If I ran, it would give chase. Standing taller, I turned around. Silence greeted me as the flickering lights cast an eerie glow on my frozen form. My heart thrashed in my chest. Where was it? Something flashed in the corner of my eyes. Out of my peripheral I could make out two beady red eyes staring at me from an alley.

My hands instinctively went to my staff, feeling its smooth wood pressed into my palm. The eyes watched me, slinking further back into the darkness. It was now or never. I faced the alley and took a shaky step into the pitch blackness. Fear tightened my chest. What if something went wrong? I shook my head. Doubt was my second handicap.

I sucked in a breath and walked deeper into the long strip. My eyes strained to see in front of my feet. I stumbled once, my shin ramming into an upturned trash can. Laughter filled my head and echoed around me. I clenched my fist around the intricate stick on my waist. Movement to my left caused me to halt. "I know you're there, just come out and face me already."

The laughter continued. "Sweet child, you better run along before misfortune befalls you," a voice whispered, sickly sweet.

Little feet pitter-pattered on the concrete. I shuddered. My palms were slick with sweat as I took out my staff. The leaf-designed wood transformed, growing in length until it was as tall as me. White energy flared off either ends of the staff. I planted my feet, ready for battle. The light from the energy blades illuminated my surroundings enough for my eyes to adjust. My body tensed. *Damn it all to hell.*

A web stretching the width of the alley blocked the path in front of me. Beads of dew were suspended on silver, silken strings along with a cocoon or two wrapped up in the fine silk. Chills ran down my spine. Arachnids. Near the top of the web sat six legs. Connected to those legs was a spider abdomen, then the torso of a woman. Long black hair flowed over her exposed breasts. Bright red eyes stared me down, a smile forming on her dark red lips.

Of all the things I could have faced today, from shadow men to incubi, it had to be one of the three spider-women.

My luck was shit. The Arachnids were known for luring men and women alike to their web and trapping them until they either died from suffocation or were drained of their life.

The three sisters - Ara, Chi, and Nida — were known throughout the Other World to terrorize humans and the three clans. History of the supernatural world hadn't been my priority at the time — I had just wanted to fit into the human world. A skill my mother prided herself on, which was a lot harder when I turned eighteen, the age a banshee has her first Death Call, premonition of a banshee's love's death. Remy knew everything that had happened back then, and knew why all hell had broken loose when I sort of let out all the people and creatures from the Abyss, a void in space.

I sighed. I just wished it wasn't this creature who I had to face. From what I had learned, there was only one sister left — the other two had been burned alive. Ara, the eldest Arachnid, loomed over me. A thousand beady red eyes glared in my direction from the alley floor. Tiny spiders crawled silently, scuttling every which way. Thank god I had worn my combat boots. The air crackled with energy. I crouched low and charged, swinging my bow staff back and forth like a sickle. Screams and hisses bounced off the walls as I cut down the number of spiders.

"How dare you hurt my children!" Ara shrieked.

I tensed, slashing at the spiders. Something whizzed by me. I stumbled backwards. My back squished into something soft and sticky. *You've got to be kidding me!* I pulled myself forward only to be yanked back again. I glanced over my shoulder and noticed that I had somehow gotten trapped in one of her webs.

The strands clung to my clothes, making it impossible to move. I clutched my staff and flipped it with a flick of my wrist. The searing energy sliced through the web with ease. I did the same on my other side until I was back on my feet again. A collective hiss reverberated through the alley. I took a deep breath and charged once more, hacking away at the swarming mass of spiders. Once again something whizzed by me.

Was she spitting silk at me? There was no time to think on it as a silver mass sailed toward me and slammed into my arm. My staff flew out of my hand and clattered to the ground. Panic spiked up my chest. My eyes locked onto Ara's. She smirked, showing off fangs glistening with a liquid I could only assume was venom.

Damn it, Remy! If he hadn't insisted on me fixing my mistakes, I wouldn't be in this mess right now.

"Sweet child, why fight me? It is a pointless endeavor. You are a fly trapped in my web. Close your eyes darling, everything will be over shortly." Her soothing voice played with my senses.

I could give in, die peacefully, and be with Kaelin again. Just the idea of it made me want to close my eyes and surrender. What I wouldn't give to see his face again, to hear his rumbling laughter, or breathe in the smell of the woods in autumn mixed with worn leather.

If I thought hard enough, I could catch the slightest hint of it. Kaelin. My eyes drifted shut.

"That's it child, just let go and be free." A humming started in my head — soft at first but grew louder. *"Aislin! Don't give up, I'm not worth it."*

Kaelin? I shook my head. That wasn't possible. The humming intensified, adding pressure to my skull. I winced.

"Damn it Linny, open your eyes!"

My eyes snapped open just in time to catch the glint of venom on the spider-woman's fangs. There was no time to think about the voice as her mouth loomed inches away from my neck. Why the hell did everything want to bite my neck? I needed to think fast if I was going to get out of this alive. What the hell was I thinking? Dying wouldn't solve anything, not now.

Playing dead wouldn't work, and I didn't have my staff anymore, which left hands and feet. Grinding my teeth, I clenched my hand into a fist and pulled it back before letting it go. My fist hit her square in the face. She reeled back, loosening her grip around me.

Without a second thought, I jumped backwards. My feet skidded on the ground and pain throbbed up my arm from the punch. I shook it out and concentrated on finding my staff. My eyes landed on the intricate leaf design on the sides of the stick. I somersaulted to the right and grabbed it before launching to my feet again.

"You ungrateful pest! I offered you a quick death and this is how you repay me?"

I stood up and gripped the stick as it morphed into my staff once more. "Not today, bitch. I have things to do before my time comes."

Ara screeched, running toward me, her feet quick as lightning. I dodged to the left, just barely avoiding one of her barbed legs. If I was going to finish this, I needed to do it quickly. The spider hissed, coming at me once more. Her legs clicked on the asphalt. I was ready this time.

Her legs swiped again. I leaned back and struck upwards—slicing into her abdomen then down across her legs. The smell of burnt hair and flesh entered my nose. She screamed, flailing backwards. I advanced and stabbed my staff into her chest, flicking it upwards—splitting her in two.

Black blood oozed and bubbled out of her mouth. I cover my nose and stepped back. With a sigh, I pulled out my phone and called Remy.

"Hey, it's done. Can you teleport me back?"

He coughed on the other line. "Um, well . . . you see . . ."

I cut him off. "You can't, can you? Figures."

"I wish I could Aislin, but I can't actually teleport people. It's different with objects because I can just do a relocation spell."

"Yeah, yeah, it's fine. I'll find my own way back." I ended the call before he could say anymore.

I shoved my phone into my back pocket, thankful it hadn't gotten smashed in the fight. Now then, how the hell was I getting back? I rummaged in my jean pockets for cash. *You've got to be kidding me.* Nothing. There went the cab ride.

Just my luck. Stuck in a city, smelling like god knows what, not to mention looking like straight up hell. What could be worse? Something cold and wet hit my face. I glanced up and was met with another drop. The universe hated me, that's all I could think. Rain fell softly, washing away some of the blood on my jeans and jacket.

I pulled my hood up and stuffed my hands into my pockets. This night was just getting better and better. I shuffled back out of the alley. The light from the moon was shrouded by rain clouds. The street was grey and gloomy— the perfect atmosphere for how I was feeling.

~ ~ ~

Water dripped as I walked to Remy's office. I flung open the door. It slammed against the wall. Remy's brown eyes widened at the sight of me.

"Oh my. Y-You're soaking wet."

I glared at him. "No shit, Sherlock. It's been raining for the past hour, and thanks to you I had to walk in it."

He frowned, pushing up his glasses. "Surely you could have called a cab or something. For Pete's sake, you're going to wind up catching a cold. Here, take this." He tossed his jacket across the room. It flopped at my feet.

"I'm fine," I grumbled, "I just wanted to tell you I killed the beast, and for your information it was a damn Arachnid."

Remy laced his fingers together and rested his chin on his hands. "Hmm, that would explain the lack of blood and the shriveled bodies of the victims. Ara was known for her massacres and disregard of secrecy. She didn't particularly care who knew what she was or did."

I crossed my arms over my drenched jacket, ignoring the one on the floor. "Yeah, well, thanks for the heads up. I was almost spider food."

A chuckle escaped before Remy could cover it with a cough, sinking lower into his hands. "But you weren't, so shouldn't we be celebrating your victory?" He glanced down at the puddle growing at my feet. "You should probably change first though."

I rolled my eyes, catching a shadow of a smile on his lips. Despite it all, I wouldn't change my decision to release everyone from the Abyss. They weren't all bad — some like Remy were wrongly accused. Hell, I had even been stuck there. I shivered. It wasn't a place I would want to go back to any time soon.

The cold, dark, in-between world was nothing short of torture. It had been like floating in space, blind and unable to touch or feel anything. Screams and moans of the other accused could be heard, but that was it — only my thoughts and their cries. Never again. Anything was better than that place.

"All right, I'll be back in a few. It had better be worth it this time, Remy — no cheap-ass meal." I turned on my heels and stomped out of the room, my shoes squeaking with each step. A trail of wet footprints marked my path.

Chapter 3

Kaydynce

"My queen, the time is almost upon us."

I glanced up from my nails and fixed my gaze on the pixie in front of me. Iridescent wings twitched, casting rainbows on the empty throne room. Its tiny hands fidgeted, clasping and unclasping its fingers. Light flickered in and out, bouncing off its wings.

The room was covered in windows, allowing the last rays of sun to touch the white wall to the left. The floors were alabaster with flecks of gray in the marbled tiles. My castle, my kingdom — it was all mine. I was queen of the Otherworld, and Illium was my king. We had won the war on the old king. The corners of my lips lifted at the memory.

"Are you ready, my lady? We can wait if you wish."

I shook my head. There was no way I was leaving now, not when I was so close to having everything I wanted. I glanced at the man beside me. Long silver hair flowed down his back as indigo eyes scrutinized my every move. Illium — the man who had changed my life forever.

An army of love-struck creatures stood behind me, ready to give their lives, though not truly willing. A grin spread across my lips. I had done that - entranced everyone with a mere touch. With the powers I had, no one could stop us. Lightning flashed. I jumped back. Strong arms wrapped around my waist.

"We have been seen, my lady. We must act now if we want to win."

He was right — it was now or never. I squared my shoulders and sauntered through the huge wooden doors. Chaos rained down around us. Fire, water, wind — any element I could think of was thrown around, slamming into unsuspecting victims. Excitement bubbled up inside of me - I wanted to join the fray. Illium led me to one of the farthest walls.

"Stay here, your job is done. Now let me finish this and soon we will walk these halls together." Cool lips brushed against mine and just as quickly were gone.

Metal clashed, sparks flew, and angry screams and roars echoed off the walls. I watched Illium dash into the fray. Fear clutched my chest. The body count was accumulating, and blood was everywhere. The once white marble floors were splashed red, black, and blue with the blood of both sides. My hands itched to fight. Creatures of all kinds fought around me, and I was just standing on the sidelines.

Silver rushed in front of me. Without thinking, I grabbed for it. My fingers wrapped around a slim wrist. The creature screamed, whirling on me. Crimson red eyes glared down at me, fangs flashing.

"How dare you? Who the hell do you think you are?" Energy pulsed around us, but I didn't let go.

The vampire's tone spiked my anger and hunger called to me. I grinned. I felt a stirring in my stomach and I licked my lips.

"I'm your next queen . . . though you won't be living much longer to see it."

She laughed, her eyes glowing. "I doubt that. Our king is all powerful. I may die, but he will live forever."

Lightning flashed to our right as a piercing cry reverberated through the hall. Everyone froze. I glanced toward the noise.

Illium stood on the dais, a staff held in his right hand. Energy swirled around him, his white hair lifting. Crouched before him was a puny man with short yellow hair and a billowing coat. The corners of my lips lifted as my hand caressed up her arm. Blue tendrils of energy snaked and curled, following my touch.

"Your king is nothing," I whispered, "compared to mine."

The vamp's face softened, and her eyes turned a light blue. I closed my eyes, enjoying the high of knowing I could control her. Leaning close, I brushed my lips against her pale pink ones. She sighed, pressing closer. My fingers tightened on her arm. Her essence tasted like fire and brimstone with a kick of spice. It didn't take long for her life to end. With a snap of my fingers, it was over.

Her body crumbled to the ground, drained of everything. Power flowed through me. I wobbled, suddenly unstable. I had forgotten about the side-effect of using my succubus powers. Being only half banshee and half succubus meant draining lifeforces completely weakened me instead of making me stronger. I clutched the wall and waited for my king. Silence filled the chambers. The battle was over, and we had won. I sighed. Illium and Kaydynce, rulers of the Otherworld.

I grinned, thinking about that victory, but reality pulled me back. *Time, oh that's right.*

"Ugh, I don't understand why I've had to wait a whole year. How long does it take to find one person?" I tapped my fingers on the arm of my chair. Illium sighed.

"Patience, my queen. You will have all that you desire in due time." He laid his hand over mine. I snatched my perfectly manicured hand away and glared at him. Silence filled the chambers.

"I don't want it in due time — I want it now! I've waited long enough. Where the hell is my Kaelin?"

Illium's indigo eyes narrowed as he pursed his pale lips. I smirked, knowing just the mention of Kaelin grated on his nerves. Those lips tempted me with their scold.

"My queen tests my own patience." The warm air turned suddenly frigid, and I shivered. "For me to find your *precious Kaelin*, I need a tracker. Sadly, the only known one was killed, but my sources tell me there may be a way to retrieve said tracker. The catch, my lovely, is I must enact one of my favors from your dear friend, Aislin."

I crossed my arms over my chest and turned away. Ugh, Aislin was the whole reason Kaelin was gone. When I had heard the news, I couldn't believe it. Kaelin dead? The mere thought had been brushed off. There had been no way he could have died.

That was when I put the pieces together — Death Calls and what happens when one is received. The warning signs had been there, but who paid attention to them anyway? It was all her fault. Aislin had stolen Kaelin away from me. At least she'd gotten what she'd deserved.

"Isn't there another way?" I asked, pouting.

Illium brushed away a stray blond hair from my face. I closed my eyes and leaned into his touch. Coldness seeped into my skin.

"This isn't a normal favor. Aislin plans to enter the Underworld, or Hell as you would call it. It is a dangerous endeavor, which you may find appealing – Aislin will suffer. She must overcome many obstacles."

"Yeah, yeah—what does this have to do with the favor?" A smirk played across his lips. "The tracker is in Hell."

My eyes widened as my mouth formed an O. "That's perfect, though I don't understand why it would take a fricking year."

"The one you call Remy had to prepare the necessary ingredients and prep Aislin for the journey ahead. It is not something to be taken lightly. Extreme amounts of magic are required to even be able to open the gates of Hell, much less send someone through it. Time here is not the same as the human world, as you already know. What is one more day here—three days, a week over there?"

"Whatever, as long as I get my Kaelin back."

Illium nodded, his long white hair moving in time with him. He was right though. Time moved slower in the Otherworld. A month here was like three or four back home. An ache formed in my chest. I hadn't seen my grandma since the trial. I wondered if she was doing okay. Pain laced up my sides and I sucked in a breath. The gnawing hunger had begun. I scanned the room, my eyes latched onto a retreating form.

"You there, come closer," I called.

The pixie froze in her tracks and turned slowly. Silver eyes widened. Her small frame shook with each step. Silver hair flowed down her back just past her shimmering wings.

"Y-Yes, my queen?"

I studied the fey, licking my lips. She would do nicely. I extended a finger and beckoned her closer until she was only inches away from me. Her tiny heart pounded. Excitement bubbled up. I hadn't fed in what felt like ages.

"What is your name?" I asked, my voice turning sickly sweet.

"I-It's Blithe, my queen. H-Have I done something wrong?"

I didn't answer. Fear rolled off Blithe in waves. I inhaled its delicious scent.

"Blithe here is the keeper of time," Illium informed.

I smiled and brushed a finger down her pale cheek. Warmth flooded through me. The girl sighed, her heartbeat returning to normal. My finger travelled down her cheek to her chin and lifted it slightly. I leaned in and lightly grazed my lips on hers and breathed in her essence. Blue tendrils swirled around us. I devoured it greedily. Vanilla and honey, light and airy — delicious.

"Kaydynce." The warning tone snapped me back to reality. I gasped, pushing the pixie away.

Blithe crumbled to the marble floor, her pulse quiet. I closed my eyes for a second and calmed my own thrashing heart.

"Take her out of my sight."

"Your wish is my command, my queen." Illium shuffled passed me and lifted the girl into his arms. With a wave of his hand, a portal opened out of thin air. He turned, a glint in his purple eyes. "I shall be back."

I nodded and watched him vanish from sight. My shoulders slumped as I leaned back in my chair. What had gotten into me? I admit, control wasn't my strong suit, but that still didn't explain the desire to drain the pixie dry. The hunger had been so strong, crippling even, but I knew I hadn't wanted to kill her because I was hungry.

I shivered. I wanted her dead because she was pretty. Anger and hurt swirled in my head. I clenched my fist. *Damn you, Aislin. You are the cause of all my problems.* The corners of my lips lifted in a dark smirk. *Watch your back Aislin, because I'm coming for you.*

Chapter 4

Aislin

"Achoo." I sniffed, wiping my nose with my sleeve. A chill ran up my spine. *Weird.* I shook it off.

Remy raised a brow. "Are you okay?"

I smiled, rolling my eyes. "I'm fine, just a sneeze. I'm not getting sick, don't worry — though it wouldn't surprise me since you made me walk in the rain."

He sputtered, his eyes widening. His glasses fell to the bridge of his nose. "T-That's not fair. I-I didn't make you walk."

I chuckled. "I'm just messing with you."

His cheeks turned a light shade of pink. *Still as shy as ever.* The tantalizing aroma of food drifted toward us and my mouth watered. When was the last time I'd eaten? I couldn't remember, but my stomach sure did. It gurgled and rumbled in response.

My eyes drifted around the tiny restaurant. Knickknacks of all kinds were displayed on the walls, from antique Coke bottles to signs from the 50's. The place was on the outskirts of town. It attracted enough business to survive, but not enough to renovate.

The little dive had maybe twelve tables in all. A small bar stood to the back of the restaurant, the counter curving into a C. Stools were placed haphazardly around it. I was surprised when Remy had suggested the diner. It wasn't a big hangout spot, which was probably why he'd picked it in the first place. I glanced over the menu, undecided.

"Hey Remy, you want your usual today?" A petite server asked, sauntering up to our table. I raised a brow.

"N-No thank you, Joy. I-I'll just have a chicken sandwich with a side of fries and a Coke." A light pink blush flooded his cheeks once again.

The girl giggled then turned to me, her brown eyes narrowing. "And what can I get you?"

I fidgeted under her glare. "Um, can I have a cheeseburger with ketchup and mayonnaise with a side of fries? Oh, and a sweet tea, please."

She nodded, jotting it down. Her ponytail bounced with her movement. "I'll be back with y'all's drinks." She sashayed off.

The minute she was gone, I turned and glared at Remy. "W-What?"

I crossed my arms over my chest. "Oh nothing, just that I got the evil eye from *Joy*."

"Oh." He bowed his head. "Sorry. I usually come here by myself."

"You should know better." A smile played across my lips. "I think she has a crush on you."

His head snapped up, eyes widening. "T-That can't be true." He paused, glancing down again. "Even if she does—I couldn't—it wouldn't be right."

I reached over the table and rested a hand on his shoulder. "Nereida would understand. She would want you to be happy."

He sighed, shoulders slumping. "I know you're right. I just don't know how to be happy without her. She was the only light in my life, and I lost her in a blink of an eye. Her death will always be on my hands."

Nereida, the daughter of Remy's previous master and a mermaid, had been the love of his life, but had died tragically—fighting a war she should have never been involved in to begin with. Remy had seen it all. Filled with rage and sorrow, his powers had manifested. Before he could do anything, the Court found him and sent him to the Abyss.

I shook my head. "You can't think like that. It wasn't your fault. She knew what she was getting herself into when she rode into that village."

"Yeah. But if I had been a little bit faster, maybe I could have saved her, or taken the bullet instead."

"Fate is a bitch."

Remy nodded in agreement. I sat back in my seat. Joy came back moments later with our drinks. She didn't say a word, just walked away.

"I think we pissed her off." I chuckled under my breath.

Remy ran a hand down his face.

"Hey, don't worry, she'll forgive you—eventually," I joked, waiting for a response.

He frowned. "That's not the issue right now. It's what I brought you here to discuss." He shook his head. "If what my source says is true, facing Hell won't be our only problem."

I raised a brow. "Okay. You need to give me a little more information than that. I'm not a mind reader, you know."

"It would be a lot easier if you were." He took a deep breath before meeting my quizzical stare. "The King of the Otherworld has been defeated."

"Um, is that supposed to mean something to me?" *King of the Otherworld?*

Remy closed his eyes, pinching the bridge of his nose with his thumb and his forefinger.

"Sometimes I forget you were raised not knowing much about the other side. Let me break it down for you. The Otherworld was a peaceful land where the supernatural originally lived. It wasn't until the vampires crossed over to the human world that disagreements arose.

"The Esor Animis, soul-eaters clan and the Nocturna Suppressions, nightmares clan thrived on fear and their encounters with humans. The Lux Lucis, the light clan wanted nothing to do with the human plane. The Lux Lucis wanted to close the gate completely, which would mean only the Lux Lucis would have the ability to conjure portals or doorways to any place or world they wanted. War broke out. The Esor Animis and Nocturna Suppressions fought side by side against the Lux Lucis. Many lives were lost that day, but ultimately the Lux Lucis won.

"To prevent further problems, the Lux Lucis elected a king to rule over them all. A staff of the elements was forged, and only a member of the Lux Lucis could wield it. Many of the

Esor Animis and Nocturna Suppressions were banished to the human world, never to see the Other World again, but some swore fealty to the king for forgiveness. That's also how the Court came to be. A chosen representative of each clan every hundred or so years to keep the Otherworld in check. The king rules over the people, the Court enforces the so-called laws. Anyways, the gateway was sealed shut . . . until now."

"Um, thanks for the history lesson Remy, but I still don't see how this is a problem."

He opened his mouth and closed it. Joy resurfaced with our food, set the plates down, grimaced, then walked away once more.

"She's a talkative one, isn't she?" Silence fell.

Remy studied his food but didn't touch it. I sighed, pushing my plate away. "All right, what's up with you?" No answer. "Fine, how does a new king affect us?"

He pushed up his glasses, his brown eyes darkening. "Any other time a new king wouldn't affect the human realm, but this time it does. It's not just the king we have to worry about. Aislin," he paused, "it's Kaydynce—she is the new queen and Illium is the new king."

My jaw dropped. Tea dripped out of my open mouth and down my chin. "What?"

"This is only if my source is correct. But alas, I don't doubt her word. That's not even the worst of it."

Not the worst of it? "What could possibly be worse than those two ruling a world?" I picked up a fry to nibble on it.

"Ruling another, especially now that the gateway to the Human Realm is open."

My hand stilled, dropping the fry I'd picked up on my lap. "Please tell me you're not saying what I think you're saying."

He bowed his head. "Illium plans to enslave all humanity and rule over them. Humans would become a food source."

"You've got to be kidding me." I leaned back in my seat. "That's absurd! Is that even possible?"

"Nothing is impossible. I wouldn't put it passed Illium—he seemed shifty from the beginning, but Kaydynce?" Remy shook his head.

"Kaydynce has changed. I don't even know her anymore." My shoulders slumped.

The girl I'd grown up with was gone. No more trips to the mall or talking about boys. So much had changed in less than a year. Stillness settled over us once more. Thoughts drifted in and out of my mind. I would have to fight her.

My best friend was now my enemy. Chills ran up my spine. If all of it was true, then I'd lost more than I had first assumed. Three friends in a year—gone. I pushed my plate away again, my appetite spoiled.

Chapter 5

Aislin

Speak of the devil and he shall appear . . . well, it took a couple days, but the concept still stood.

~ ~ ~

I ducked under a right swing and punched low. Remy blocked and skidded backwards. After the whole restaurant conversation a few days ago, I'd needed to relieve stress. Fighting was my outlet. Taking my stance again, I prepared for the next hit, but it never came. A shimmering archway had opened in front of us. I jumped back, my heart pounding. There was only one person we knew who could open doors out of thin air: Illium. A shadow crossed in front of the bright light. I shielded my eyes. Where was he coming from? Silence filled the room. Nobody moved. I glanced at Remy. His dark eyes had turned to slits. Energy buzzed as tensions grew.

Illium's willowy frame stepped out from the entrance. Indigo eyes twinkled the minute he spotted us. What now? Why the hell had he shown up now of all times?

"Illium. Just the person I didn't want to see today." I crossed my arms over my chest.

He bowed. Long white hair covered his face for a second. "Miss Aislin, it's so good to see you. It's been a while."

"Not long enough," I said under my breath. Illium's eyes narrowed, but he kept a smile on his face. "Why are you here,

Illium? I would think you would have better things to do than bug us."

His smile widened. Chills ran down my spine. "I've come for my end of the bargain. I hope you have not forgotten our deal we made after I saved your precious Kaelin," he spat. I flinched.

"No, I haven't forgotten . . . even though you didn't keep your end of the bargain. Kaelin is gone, but I'm going to bring him back."

Illium chuckled. "On the contrary, Miss Aislin, I did exactly what was asked of me. I kept him safe until you could bring him home—nothing more, nothing less. Kaelin being killed is not my problem."

My jaw clenched. I sucked in a deep breath and let it out slowly. "It damn well is." My hands balled into fists. "You were supposed to keep the Court away from us, but instead they went and killed him. This is all your fault! He would still be alive if you'd kept your end of the deal!" My voice rose with each word. Tears streamed down my cheeks.

Remy rested a hand on my shoulder. I leaned into him, glaring at the man who had inevitably killed my love. Illium's whole demeanor changed in an instant. The room became frigid. Ice formed on the mirror to my left. I shivered. His indigo eyes turned violet. Shit. He took a step closer, a dark shadow crossing his pale face. If there was ever a time to be scared, it would be now.

"I don't like this," Remy whispered. I didn't either.

"Listen closely, Aislin Gray. I have kept the Court from chasing after you as per your request. Your human was never part of the equation. I will excuse your behavior and accusations only because I have need of you and your wizard friend. There have been murmurs about a young banshee trying to enter the Realm of the Dead, or Hell as the humans call it. If the rumors are true, then I require a soul only you can retrieve for me."

"Wait a minute. You need me to do what?"

He sighed. "I require a soul from the Realm of the Dead."

"Okay, I get that, but why in the world would you need a soul? And to do what with?"

Illium smirked, eyes bright. "That is none of your concern. If you intend to go through with this endeavor, then I would ask you to collect this soul."

I shook my head. "You know damn well you aren't asking or else you wouldn't be here trying to collect my debt. A deal is a deal though, despite how messed up I think this is. I'll get your soul. Just tell me who and where to find them."

"I'm so glad you asked."

Remy leaned closer. "Aislin, this is a bad idea."

I sighed and glanced at Remy, shoulder slumped. "I gave my word. There's no turning back."

Illium bowed. "I'm surprised you agreed so quickly." He straightened and waved his hand across his face. "But no matter. The soul I need is of a traitorous werewolf. He is one of the best trackers around, but sadly he got caught sleeping with the Alpha's mate, then tried to fight him for dominance and lost. But I digress. It's no real concern of yours of how he got there. The only thing you need to worry about is getting him out of Lucifer's chambers."

I threw my hands up in the air. "You have got to be kidding me! Lucifer? Seriously? Of all the people in the Underworld, you want me to steal a soul from Lucifer—the devil himself?"

Illium nodded. "Exactly. I should also mention Elijah is one of his personal hellhounds."

"I'm done." I turned and walked away. There was no way I was going to steal from the devil—just no way.

"Aislin, where are you going?" Remy called out. I shook my head.

"There is no way out of this, Aislin. A deal is a deal." Ignoring them both, I pushed open the doors to the outside world. Fresh air was what I needed.

Ice sliced through me. The frigid air calmed my frayed nerves. I took a step down onto the sidewalk. Rain pitter pattered on the concrete. Closing my eyes, I lifted my face to the sky. Cold water droplets splashed and traveled down my cheeks.

What the hell was Illium thinking? Retrieving Kaelin's soul was one thing, but finding and stealing another from Lucifer was a death wish. *Why does he need a tracker of all things?* I shook my head. *I'm screwed.* Maybe it would all be suicide. Prancing into Hell wasn't something sane people did. What if I couldn't find him? My chest tightened. No, I couldn't think like that. I needed to be strong for both our sakes.

Sighing, I opened my eyes and turned back. There was no use running from my problems. I needed to face them head on if I was ever going to get through it. A smug smile greeted me the minute I walked through the doors.

"I see you have come back to your senses."

My eyes narrowed. "Let's get something straight, Illium. I'm doing this to save the love of my life and complete my end of the deal—nothing else."

His violet eyes danced. "I would ask nothing less of you. In four weeks' time, you will be on your way to the pits of Hell. Are you sure you're ready?"

I gulped at his intense stare, but squared my shoulders. *Don't show fear.* "I'm as ready as I will ever be." Remy nodded, smiling slightly.

Illium took another step forward. "I thought you might say that." He bowed, his right hand over his heart while the other was extended. "If you so believe, then spar with me. I will show you what you are really up against."

My eyes shifted to Remy. His body stiffened, hands clenched at his sides. *Damn it, he's mocking us.*

"Fine," I said, capturing his gaze, "I will fight you, and I won't be going easy on you either."

Illium grinned. "I wouldn't have it any other way, Miss Aislin."

I stepped backwards and into one of my stances. My hand clasped around the leaf-designed stick that would become my bow staff if need be. Illium took his own stance and beckoned. Planting my feet, I waited for his next move.

I wasn't dumb enough to strike first—it would only leave me vulnerable. Quick as lightning, he struck. In a matter of seconds, he was inches away from my face. I froze.

"How do you expect to fight when you can't even move from fear?" he whispered. The scent of fresh mint drifted up my nose.

I stumbled backwards, my heart racing. My grip on the smooth wood of my staff tightened, but I didn't pull it out. Illium's smirk widened. I sucked in a shaky breath and stood my ground. Losing wasn't an option. He nodded and advanced. I saw his movements this time and dodged to the right. He followed suit, attacking from the right. I tumbled out of range, barely avoiding his fists.

"I see you are capable of defense, but what about offense?"

My body tensed. He was right. Defense was my norm because I was rarely ever offensive. Without a second thought, I charged. Illium stood still. Odd. I didn't have time to think of his reasoning. Fists raised, I struck.

My punch collided with his arms, which were positioned into an X. The energy of the hit vibrated up my arm. I jumped back and attacked once more. A right swing to the jaw— he dodged, a low kick to the knees—he skidded away, and finally a double punch to the gut. Illium held his abdomen.

"Very good. I see you have grown since I last saw you fight." His eyes shifted to my waist. He frowned. "What, might I ask, is that on your hip?"

I followed his gaze to my staff. "Oh this?" I unsheathed it. The minute my fingers grazed the intricate patterns, it transformed into my bow staff.

Illium's lips turned down further. He took a step closer and reached out with shaking hands. I raised a brow. The staff was about as tall as me, maybe more, with blades of white energy at both ends. Vines and leaves covered the length of the smooth wood.

"How did you come to obtain such a weapon?"

My chest clenched. "The Court member who killed Kaelin had it. It was a broad sword when she held it. She plunged it through my stomach and left me for dead. When

I pulled it out, it became what you see now—my bow staff."

"Beautiful and deadly. The weapon you possess is an elven blade of energy that changes its form based on the wielder. It's known as Lassemaica, which translates to Leaf Blade, for the designs on the hilt. I had no inkling that Seraphina possessed such a weapon. May I hold it?" He held out a pale hand.

I hesitated. What would happen if he acquired this weapon? Sighing, I handed it over. His fingers wrapped around the wood. In a blink of an eye, it morphed into a jagged dagger. The edges were curved with a violet energy that pulsed with heat. My eyes widened. Illium tossed it from hand to hand.

"This is quite a magnificent weapon. Keep it close—or someone might steal it right from under your nose."

"I'll keep that in mind, thank you." The corners of his lips lifted slightly.

He extended the blade, palm open. I cautiously wrapped my fingers around the hilt. His hand fell back to his side. Silence crept in around us.

Illium bowed. "I shall take my leave then, as my business here is finished. When the time comes for your departure, I will be here to see you off."

"How thoughtful of you," I said sarcastically. If I never saw his face again, it would be too soon.

He chuckled, lifting a hand and snapped his fingers. An outline of a door shimmered into existence, a bright light filtering through. I shielded my eyes. Before I could blink, he was gone.

"Thank God." Remy sighed, running a hand down his face. "I thought he would never leave."

"Yeah, well, he'll be back, unfortunately." I closed my eyes and took a deep, calming breath.

"You know you don't have to do this if you don't want to." He rested a hand on my shoulder.

I opened my eyes and turned, smiling at Remy. "I know, but I'm not giving up on him, not now, not ever. Which means I have to go down the rabbit hole."

He nodded. "All right, I'm behind you in every way. I may not know Kaelin like you do, but I'll do everything in my power to bring him back."

"Thanks, if all goes well I'll see him again—I just hope he's still the same Kaelin that I knew."

Chapter 6

Aislin

The days dragged on after Illium's visit. Tensions were high. The year had flown by in a blink of an eye. I wasn't the same girl I had been when I'd started this endeavor. Would Kaelin notice the changes? I shook my head. There was no point dwelling in uncertainties—he either would or wouldn't. My world had crumbled around me last year, and now was the time to pick up the pieces again.

Sucking in a breath, I pushed open the door to Remy's study. The sun had set not long before, painting the sky in reds, pinks, and oranges. Snores drifted through the now open door, bouncing off the bookshelves. A grin spread across my lips.

Remy was passed out in his chair, one arm behind his head and his legs crossed on his desk. It didn't seem comfy, but who was I to judge? There was no reason to wake him. It was late, and he needed his sleep more than ever if he was going to create a portal to Hell in the upcoming week.

I yawned, fighting sleep. It seemed as if I was getting back later and later from rounding up the creatures I had let loose a year ago. My birthday had come and gone. No point in celebrating it when my eighteenth birthday had caused so much pain and loss. Thinking back on it, both Teagan's and Kaydynce's birthdays had passed—neither of whom were here to celebrate. My roots were coming into play. All things happen in threes—three visions of death, and now three friends gone. Two were dead, and the third might as well be.

I still couldn't believe Kaydynce was my enemy now, after everything we had been through. It didn't matter anymore. My feet shuffled back to my makeshift bed against the far wall of the training area. I flopped into bed and wrapped myself up in the blanket and let sleep take over.

~ ~ ~

The light flickered in the distance, casting shadows on the pavement. Pavement? Where was I? Laughter filled my ears. Pain sliced up my body. The night caved in around me. I held my stomach. A warm liquid spread between my fingers. The air buzzed with electricity, sending chills down my spine. This wasn't right. Two figures appeared before me—one laid crumpled on the ground while the other towered over him. *No, this wasn't happening—not again.*

"Kaelin!" I screamed, but no sound came out. I was too late—just like last time.

"You'll never save him," a sickly-sweet voice whispered. It wasn't true. *I'm not losing him again.*

Lightning flashed, illuminating the killer. Blonde hair cascaded around her shoulders and framed her face and dark blue eyes. I stumbled backwards. No, this wasn't right—this wasn't how it happened.

"N-No, Seraphina killed him—not you."

Kaydynce smiled a glint to her eyes. "You wish it had been me so you wouldn't have to deal with me anymore." She pouted her lips. "You always hated me for what I did to him."

I shook my head. "Of course not! You were my friend, despite everything."

Kaydynce scoffed. "Was, but not anymore, right?"

"This is just a dream—a figment of my imagination."

"You can't escape the truth," she hissed before vanishing in a puff of smoke.

Darkness caved in until the only light came from the street lamp a few feet away. Kaelin's body had also disappeared. I was left alone to my thoughts and unable to wake from this nightmare. *Wake up—I need to wake up.* The hollowness inside ever since his death pressed on my chest. Breathing became difficult.

"You should have died," a voice moaned. The hairs on my arms stood up.

It was starting again—the disembodied voices, visions of death—be it past or present, and the emptiness of knowing I couldn't do anything. A shaking started in my legs and travelled upwards until my whole body was trembling. I wanted to block it all out, or at least leave this nightmare. The darkness thickened until I couldn't even see my hands.

The Abyss had the same feeling. I was locked in a bubble, unable to see or touch—just listen to the whisperings. My chest tightened even more. Oxygen entered my lungs, but it did nothing for the constriction. Spots of reds and greens clouded my already limited vision.

Air whooshed passed me as I fell backwards. The Abyss receded.

I gasped awake, eyes flying open. My hands instinctively went to my stomach. When I looked down, nothing was amiss. It had felt so real though. The training room slowly came into focus. The sun peeked over the horizon, casting the sky in oranges and blues as the first rays of light hit the window. I shivered, rubbing my arms.

It's freezing in here. I let out a puff of air; it withered and snaked like cigarette smoke. Why was it so damn cold? Temperatures were moderate here even in winter, though there were the few cold days in between. What was today? I frowned. The days had blurred and mixed together until I didn't know how many days were left. Three . . . or was it two? Either way, the time was fast approaching.

I pushed myself up, wincing slightly. The dream may not have been real, but the pain sure as hell was. The wound from that night pulsed and throbbed as if it had just happened. Stumbling out of bed, I shuffled to Remy's office. A yawn escaped my lips. Damn, I needed coffee—the one thing that we didn't have in this building. A refrigerator? Yes. A coffee machine? Nope. The door to Remy's study was ajar. A soft light filtered through the crack. I pressed my ear to the door, checking for any sounds.

Nothing. That was odd. I pushed the door open just enough for me to squeeze through. The room was vacant. I frowned, studying everything. All his books were neatly stacked and put away—even the pile of papers on his desk were organized. Nothing was amiss except Remy. Where did he go?

"Hey Aislin, I'm surprised to see you awake."

I jumped and swiveled around, heart racing. Remy stood behind me. I hadn't even heard him approach.

"Shit, Remy, you scared the hell out of me."

He chuckled, adjusting his glasses. "Just trying to keep you on your toes." His face sobered. "You never know when you will be attacked—always be prepared for the unexpected."

I sighed. "I guess I'm screwed then."

"Not necessarily—just be aware of your surroundings and use your senses."

"Thanks, but that doesn't make me feel any better. By the way, how many days are left?"

His brows furrowed. "Aislin, time is up. Today is the day you have been waiting for since Kaelin's death. All that needs to be done is preparing the ingredients and speaking the words. Are you sure you're ready for this?"

Was I? Probably not, but there was no turning back now. "Yeah, sure. When do we begin?"

Remy glanced at the tiny clock hidden on one of the shelves. The antique thing ticked away the seconds.

"It's barely six now. When the clock hits nine, we shall begin."

I nodded. "All right, three hours it is. I suppose there isn't much else to do besides wait it out. Breakfast then? You can't be summoning portals on an empty stomach, right?"

The corners of Remy's lips turned up. "I suppose not."

I grinned and held out an arm. "Shall we?"

He hooked his arm in mine. "Lead the way, madam. I'm quite famished, if I do say so myself."

I laughed, rolling my eyes. "Okay, but you're buying."

He shook his head, smirking. "Very well, but only because I'm about to send you down to the pits of Hell." "Fair enough." *Hell. Ready or not, here I come.*

Chapter 7

Aislin

"All right, do you have everything you need?"

I nodded, patting my backpack. We weren't sure how long it would take for me to find Kaelin and this so-called tracker, so packing supplies was a necessity. Unease settled in the pit of my stomach. All my doubts resurfaced. What if I couldn't find him? What if he wasn't there? So many *what if* scenarios ran through my mind that I couldn't keep track. I took a deep breath. It was now or never.

"Okay, listen closely. I'm going to cast the spell to open the portal, and I'm going to need the Leaf Blade. When you are ready to return you can just hold it up and create your own portal. I'm hoping it won't come to that, but there is a slight possibility that it might. I can only hold the doorway open for a certain amount of time without disrupting both our world and Hell. A week is all the time I will give you before I'm coming in after you—with or without Kaelin."

"Sounds easy enough—anything else I should know?" I asked studying the candles fixed in a circle.

Silence greeted my question. It was all the answer I needed.

"I see the party has started without me."

I spun on my heels and faced Illium. Indigo eyes danced as a grin played across his lips. He was the last person I wanted to see.

"What do you want?" I crossed my arms over my chest and stared him down—or rather up.

The smirk never left his lips, if anything it widened. "I'm here just like I said I would be—to see you off, of course. I also have a bit of info you might like to hear."

"All right, I'm listening." *Might as well hear what he must say.*

He clapped his hands together. "Splendid, now then—here are some details you may not know. For instance, Hell is made up of three tiers: the first is the human version that is depicted throughout history—the whole fire and brimstone thing. The second is what most supernatural call The Underworld. This is where all the malicious creatures with souls go, along with humans who have been affected by such creatures, like your Kaelin. The last tier is where you will find my prize—Lucifer's chambers."

I glanced at Remy, fear clutching my throat. Why hadn't I known about the layers? He frowned, glasses falling down the bridge of his nose. My hands twitched at my sides. Silence crept in like the night. Seconds ticked by until a shrill beeping sounded from the alarm Remy had set. Nine o'clock had struck its first note. Illium bowed and backed up a step.

"Let the show begin."

With one last glance at Illium, I turned back to Remy—ready whenever he was. Taking my cue, he crossed his legs and plopped down on the outskirts of the candles. He held out his hand. I sucked in a breath and pulled out the Leaf Blade and placed it in his palm before backing up.

The blade instantly morphed. Instead of a sword or a dagger, it took the shape of a shield. Blue energy shrouded half his body. I stared in awe. Remy ignored the change and closed his eyes, starting to chant.

I watched, transfixed. A blue aura swirled around him, whipping and snapping in the air. This was the same guy I had saved a year ago. His appearance hadn't changed in the slightest, but his skills and confidence had. He wasn't the shy, inexperienced wizard I'd freed anymore. He had become something more.

"Aperiesque ostium ad inferni!" He yelled, lifting his arms and the blade. "Ligabis ad herba ostium!"

A sudden wind slashed at my clothes and hair. A brilliant light shot up from the circle then burst. I shielded my eyes. The blast sent waves of energy through the room, almost knocking me over. A portal of red and orange opened before us.

"It's time, Aislin," Remy yelled over the howling wind. He tossed the Leaf Blade back to me. My hands fumbled around the hilt before my fingers finally wrapped around it.

"Jump already—this is getting boring," Illium groaned.

As if on cue, a gust of wind hit my back. I went spiraling down the rabbit hole. Nothing could have prepared me for what awaited me at the bottom. Yellows, reds, and oranges blurred and shifted in my vision. Warmth spread up my body and through my veins.

The heat quickly scorched my skin. I winced, but couldn't move away for I was still falling like an endless nightmare. Thoughts of death flickered across my mind. Was this where I'd end up? Without warning, I slammed into the ground. My left side took the brunt of the hit. Pain raced up my shoulder and sides. I sucked in a shaky breath.

Muffled cries and whimpers echoed off the red hued walls. I shivered. Chills ran up and down my spine despite the suffocating heat. A drop of sweat trickled down my brow. I hadn't been here even a minute and I was already sweating. Supernatural heat, or maybe my body just couldn't handle the sudden change in temperature. The walls danced as if they were alive with flames licking their feet. The acrid scent of burning flesh filled my nostrils. I covered my mouth, gagging. Doors lined the walls, each with a different number.

My heart pounded in my chest. So this was the first level. Smoke drifted through the doors on either side of me. With each quick breath, ash coated my tongue, clogging my throat. Pulling my pack around to my front, I rummaged for something to cover my face. My fingers grazed soft fabric.

Exhaling a sigh of relief, I clutched the fabric in my hands and pulled it out. My blue tank top lay crumpled in the palm of my hand. I wrapped it around my nose and mouth quickly. Anything would help my situation.

Red and orange flames hissed and crackled, flicking out their tongues. Heat bore down from all sides. Everything around me burned and smoldered or burst into little spitfires at each turn of my head. Warmth spread up my skin.

I crinkled my nose. Even through the shirt I could smell singed hair and flesh. Pain seared up my feet. I jumped from foot to foot, the scent of burning rubber reaching my nose. Shit! My shoes were catching fire. Glancing down, I understood why.

The floor was made up of cracks and fissures like cooling lava, turning to magma. Yellow and orange slits hissed and sputtered. The ground was literally a minefield of fire and brimstone. Sweat trickled down my back and forehead. I brushed what I could off. The longer I stayed, the faster I would burn, so I ran. *Kaelin, I'm coming.* Doors blurred and shifted in my vision as I ran.

What had Illium said about the levels? My mind drew a blank. I growled, clenching my hands into fists. Of all the times to forget, it chose now—one of the most important moments. Sighing, I picked up speed.

Either way I had to get to the third level—Lucifer's chamber. The heat intensified the further I ran. The doors were endless. How the hell was I supposed to get to the next area from here? There were two options: I could keep running and hope there was an exit of some sort, or I could open one of the many doors and see where it would take me. Neither option was promising.

Closing my eyes, I picked a door at random. I opened my eyes, glancing at the number on the red door. 18. I gulped. Chills ran up and down my spine. Eighteen was the age I'd had my first Death Call. The day I saw Kaelin's death. The day I became a full-fledged banshee.

My hands shook as I reached for the knob. I sucked in a breath, wincing. The silver knob seared my fingertips. As quickly as I could, I threw open the door. The sight before me would forever be in my nightmares.

The putrid odor of burning skin and singed hair permeated throughout the room. Bile rose in the back of my throat. Bone flashed through melting flesh. Blood dripped down an arm slung over a chair, pooling just underneath.

The walls were crimson red with darker spots splattered in different areas. I shivered. Tattered clothes lay abandoned. To the right of the chair was a leg. Muscles and tendons stood stark against what was left of the appendage.

Bone protruded at the end of the calf. The edges were jagged—not a clean cut. Beady red eyes reflected the scene from another vantage point—even more grotesque than anticipated. I backed up slowly. The eyes followed my every move from the corner of the room. The creature blended into the walls, barely visible.

Other body parts were strewn across the room. My heart hammered in my ears. What had happened here? The answer was obvious once all the pieces were put together. The poor soul had been ripped apart, limb from limb. My skin crawled. If he was torn apart, then that meant—the walls. I closed my eyes. I was going to be sick. The walls were painted with the blood of the victim.

Stumbling backwards, I threw up. Acid coated my throat. My stomach clenched, emptied of its contents. The door slammed behind me. Relief flooded through me. It wasn't him. I wasn't sure how I knew, but I did. Maybe our souls were connected? Whatever the reason, it hadn't been Kaelin, and I was thankful. *What now? Another door?* I cringed at the thought. There were likely to be worse things than what I had already witnessed. *Ugh, I wish I had a map.*

I needed to know though—was he here, stuck behind one of the doors? The only option was to open as many as possible. I closed my eyes and breathed in then exhaled. Hardening my heart to the sights that I'd eventually see, I started running once more. Steam hissed and billowed around me.

The cracks glowed yellow and orange. Whatever was underneath moved at a steady pace. The fissures zigzagged across the floor. Each step broke it more. The faster I ran, the quicker it cracked and broke apart. My pulse picked up speed. Fear clutched my throat. I swallowed. Would I die here? I shook the thought away. Focus. *Kaelin, where are you?* The question lay unanswered or maybe unheard.

The doors loomed on either side, begging to be opened. *Pick me, pick me*, they seemed to say. My hand shook over the handle of door twenty-five. The knob pulsed under my fingers. The vibration reverberated up my arm.

Someone or something was alive, just waiting to be released. Without a second thought, my fingers wrapped around the slim handle, wincing at the heat, and threw it open. Nothing. It was a void—an abyss of some sort. Pitch black, shrouded in darkness. It drew me in. Bleak and lonely—was this my future?

The thought should have scared me, yet I had come to terms with the inevitable. The darkness cooed and beckoned to be filled. On their own accord, my feet crossed the threshold. The minute I passed over the line, it was over. My body was sucked in. The door slammed shut. Everything fell silent. The light of the fire dimmed until all that was left was a tiny sliver under the door. This was my end—alone in the dark. I closed my eyes. If this was it then I would accept it—my own personal hell.

Something skidded across my foot. I shivered, wrapping my arms around my body. Frigid air bit into my exposed flesh.

I backed up against the door and slid down. The light from under the door flickered.

I tucked my knees against my chest and rest my chin on the tops of my knees. It wasn't hard to accept the inevitable—forever alone. That's how it was supposed to be. A banshee could never truly be happy—we were keening women after all. Sorrow and loss was in our blood.

The bleak room seemed to get bleaker the longer I sat there. Failure dragged down my mind. My search was futile—I could never save him and never would.

"Aislin, I'm sorry." My eyes snapped open.
"Kaelin?" I whispered, my voice cracking.

"Aislin, I'm sorry." He repeated those words over and over. I covered my ears. *Forever in a loop.*

I shook my head, tears catching in my lashes. This wasn't happening. *If I didn't acknowledge it, maybe it would go away.* The walls closed in, his voice getting louder.

"This isn't real," I whimpered, rocking on my heels.

Don't listen—it's only a trick. The more I said it, the more I believed. Pushing myself up with shaky legs, I stood. Kaelin's apology played in the background, but I tuned it out. This was Hell, and I had a job to do. If I couldn't save Kaelin then I sure as hell needed to save Elijah.

The question was, how could I get to Lucifer's chamber? Or better yet, how could I get out of this room? The obvious answer was the door. My hand scrounged around for the handle in the dark. I wrapped my fingers around it and twisted, but nothing happened.

I tried once more, concentrating. The lock clicked, and the door creaked open. I rushed out. A growl emanated from the room as I left. A blast of heat slammed into my face. The brightness of the hall blinded me. I shielded my eyes.

The cracks on the floor hissed and sputtered, sending out sparks of fire. I jumped back, my eyes wide. An exit—I needed an exit. My gaze shifted left to right. Nothing—just more doors. Running hadn't helped either. For all I knew there wasn't an exit.

I was stuck. The only option was to open another door. I bit my lip. Which one though? There were endless possibilities behind each door, all unpleasant. It was no surprise though; I was in Hell after all. Pick a door, any door. Sucking it up, I turned to the door across from the one I had just left. The number eighty-one glared back at me. The silver numbers stood out against the red door.

My hand hovered over the knob, hesitant in its task. What was behind here? There was only one way to find out. Taking a deep breath, I pushed it open. A bright light shone through. Was this the exit? A warm breeze tickled my skin and lifted my hair. I took a step forward. Longing clutched my heart.

"You don't belong here," a voice hissed. I spun around, senses alert. Nothing.

"Nigh, you no human—smell different." Pain laced up my leg. I winced, stepping backwards. "Taste different too." I glanced down. A dark stain spread across my pants leg. I blinked, head buzzing. Tiny red eyes glared up at me. *When had that gotten here?* My eyelids drooped, closing slightly. A weight rested on my shoulders. The fire danced and cackled in the corner of my sagging eyelids. The voice hissed and mumbled incoherently. Why was I so tired? The red walls swirled in my vision until everything blurred together to nothingness.

Chapter 8

Aislin

Pain stabbed up my leg. I gasped awake, my eyes flying open. An empty expanse of land stood before me. A gust of wind whipped and lashed at my hair. Dead grass covered the ground—brown and brittle. Where was I? My eyes drifted upwards.

The ceiling was made up of the yellow and orange cracks I had just been standing on. My fingers grazed a blade of grass. I hissed through clenched teeth. A drop of blood fell onto the singed earth. Color burst for a moment—greens and blues.

The sight didn't last. I scrambled to my feet, wincing. The wound on my leg pulsed and throbbed. How had I gotten it? Dried blood marred my jeans along with a slit that was barely noticeable. Vague images of red eyes flashed through my mind.

I blinked, shaking my head. Either way I was here now—where ever *here* was. The dying grassland went on for as far as I could see. What part of Hell was I in? There were no doors—at all. Had I made it to the second level?

If so, then how had I gotten here? Questions swirled inside my head without a single answer. Sucking in a breath, I took the first step. The grass crunched under my shoes. I scanned the vast wasteland. Nothing stood out. My hand hovered over the Leaf Blade, ready to fight if need be. My heart pounded in my ears.

The wind nipped at my flesh. The air was cooler here. With all my senses on high alert, I crept forward. If an enemy attacked, I'd at least be ready. Though if anything did appear,

I'd see them a mile away. There were no trees to hide behind—just endless marred grass.

Nothing out of the ordinary happened. I cautiously walked, waiting for something—anything to transpire. Where were all the supernatural creatures? This was Hell after all, so why a damn field? I shook my head. It seemed illogical. The further I went, the more confused I became. The grassland seemed to go on and on. The dark and dismal colors remained—greys, browns, and blacks. The flash of color I had seen before was like a faraway dream. This place was lifeless. My shoulders sagged. Was this where Kaelin had ended up or was he somewhere worse?

Neither thought helped the situation. I needed to get out of this place—I was running out of time. *Find Kaelin, find Elijah—that's all I have to do.* Both were easier said than done. I breathed in deep then let it go. My resolve was set. I trudged onward.

Silence filled my ears. Even the crunch of the grass under my feet had disappeared. The wind died down, sending chills up my arms. The stillness taunted me. I tightened my grip on the Leaf Blade.

The land sloped suddenly, catching me off guard. My foot slipped on a loose rock. I tumbled forward. My body curled into a tight ball as I rolled down the hill. The moment I stopped, I took a shaky breath. Pain raced up my sides.

I winced. A bruised rib was better than anything broken—hopefully that's all it was. I pushed myself up on wobbly legs. The scenery had changed once more. Instead of dead grass—old, rundown houses stood in front of me. I blinked. Of all the things to find in this God forsaken place, I had found a rickety town.

Just like with the grassland, there were no colors. Ivy clung to each house, wrapping around them like boa constrictors. Shattered windows, shingles falling off, and pieces of wood were missing from the exterior. Some even had broken picket fences surrounding their yards.

On shaky legs, I stumbled forward—eyes taking in everything. Who could possibly live here? A bell tolled in the background. I stopped in my tracks. It echoed like a lone cry. Goosebumps rose on my arms. The hair on the nape of my neck stood up. Boards creaked and squeaked. My heart pounded in my ears.

"Who goes there?" A voice called out.

At first I didn't see anyone. Someone huffed then a being appeared before me. I jumped back, hand at the ready on the Leaf Blade.

"Are you deaf? I asked who you are." Silver eyes squinted behind rounded glasses.

"Um, I'm Aislin, Aislin Gray."
Silver hair bounced as the apparition nodded. "I see.

Well dear, you're not supposed to be here. It's not your time."

"I-I know—I'm here searching for someone. I just don't know if he is here or not."

Pale lips turned up. "Well, maybe I can help you."

Hope fluttered. "Really, you would do that for me?"

Her eyes twinkled. "For a price, of course. I'm sure we can come to some kind of agreement."

I bit my lip. Making deals wasn't my strong suit. Look where it got me—trying to steal a soul from Hell.

"Name your price."

The woman smiled, revealing sharp, pointed teeth. I backed up, tripping over my own feet.

"Don't be afraid, child. All I want is a little taste." She licked her lips. "It's been ages since I've sunk my teeth into real flesh and bone. Spirits are one thing, but the living taste so much sweeter."

I shook my head. "No deal."

Her silver eyes narrowed. "You would say no even if it means losing the one you're searching for?"

My grip tightened on the blade. "I'll find him on my own. No deal."

"Regardless, I will have what I want!" she screeched. Her body sailed through the air toward me.

I jerked back, unsheathing my blade. I sliced upward. The end of my bow staff met flesh, searing into it. She hissed, rearing back. Black blood oozed from the wound. The woman slunk away, silver eyes glaring daggers. I let out the breath I had been holding.

Drops of blood bubbled on the ground, creating a path where the woman had gone. The beads didn't last long. Color burst once more, illuminating the shambled houses into their original forms before disappearing again.

I needed to get out of here. Grey leaves crunched under my shoes as I crept forward. I flinched at each snap. Stealth was another thing I wasn't good at. I kept the Leaf Blade out as a precaution. Better to be safe than sorry. The bell tolled again, echoing through the shacks. Shattered windows shook.

The hairs on my arms stood on end. Silence followed. My heart crashed against my chest. I picked up my pace. The sooner I left the better. The question was how. The houses stretched on for miles, with no end in sight. Maybe there were stairs downwards in one of the houses, which meant I had to enter some. I gulped.

It was now or never. Squaring my shoulders, I pressed toward the nearest one. The steps creaked under my feet. The porch was sturdier except for a few holes in the planks. The door sat ajar. The paint chipped and peeled, or at least what I hoped was paint.

I shivered, running my hands up and down my arms. *Kaelin—I'm doing this for Kaelin.* I took a deep breath then trudged onwards. The door squeaked as I pushed it open a bit more. Darkness met me head-on. The only light was the white energy blades of the Leaf Blade. It wasn't much to work with.

The place was just as vacant on the inside as it was on the outside. Books lay scattered on the floor, pages ripped out of some. Dust hung in the air. Each room appeared the same. There was no life or essence in the house.

A heavy sadness clung to the building—sucking up whatever happiness there was. The darkness loomed closer. I swung my bow staff, both blade ends lighting the room for a second or two. *Get out*, my instincts screamed. I backed up slowly. My shoulder bumped against the doorframe. I turned on my heels and ran.

"Aislin?"

I stopped dead in my tracks. It couldn't be. Of all the people to find here, it had to be him. Aaron, Teagan's second love. Images flashed through my mind: Teagan's scream and her flying at Kaydynce, his body falling to the ground, and Kaelin crouched over him.

Our eyes had met for a second before I cast my eyes away. His death had been a catalyst for everything that happened afterwards. There before me stood Aaron. Even in this colorless place I knew it was him—Kaelin's best friend and Teagan's second love.

He shuffled toward me, pushing up his glasses. My heart thumped in my ears. What would he say? Accusations? I wasn't prepared for this, but I should have figured. After all, Kaydynce did kill him. I stood, paralyzed. My hands shook. Silence followed his steps.

"Is it really you?" he asked then paused for a second, "Y-you're not dead, right?"

His body weaved in and out of existence like Teagan's had after she reached a banshee's true form. A ghost in essence. My chest tightened.

"Yes, it's me, and no, I'm not dead. I'm trying to find someone."

He nodded before frowning. "Who are you searching for?"

I bit my lip. Should I tell him? Maybe it wasn't the best time. *Yeah, I'm looking for Kaelin, you know, your best friend.* That probably wouldn't go over well.

"Um, a werewolf—he goes by the name Elijah. He's said to be one of the best trackers." A half-truth was better than a lie—right?

Aaron's face paled, or went as pale as a ghost's face could.

"W-Why do you want to find him?"

"Ugh, he's part of a deal, but that's not really important now. I'm assuming you know who I'm talking about. Do you know where he is?"

"I-I don't know anything." His body winked in and out.

I studied him, squinting my eyes. "I think you're lying, but that's okay. I wasn't looking for your help anyways. I guess I'll just be leaving." I took a step forward.

He materialized in front of me. I jumped back. "W-Wait, before you go—I have to know. Teagan—how is she?"

I gulped. That was the last question I wanted to answer. What could I say?

"Um, she's good. I don't really see her as much anymore."

He nodded. "I see, well I'm glad." Aaron smiled, face glowing before vanishing.

I sighed. God, I hoped she was in a better place. Teagan had lost enough, two loves already, hopefully she was at peace wherever she was. Thankfully she wasn't here. No more worries, Teagan was finally free. She had shed her cocoon and became a butterfly. A full banshee.

I closed my eyes. *I miss you, Teagan.*

Chapter 9

The air hummed around me, whispering in a language I couldn't understand. The more distance I put between myself and the run-down village, the louder the wind became. Loose strands of hair whipped and lashed at my face.

The temperature dropped. Puffs of smoky breath collected in front of me. I shivered. A path snaked and weaved. Blades of dead grass poked out from patches in the ground.

The landscape shifted with each step. The fields and ransacked houses disappeared, and, in their place, rocks formed. The blacks, browns, and grey scenery stayed the same. Rocks of every shape and size lined the dusty path.

Some were stacked on top of each other while some remained solitary. I wasn't sure how long I had been walking. Time was nonexistent here. What could have been a few minutes felt like an hour or more. There were no apparent changes in the sky. The crackling reddish-orange fissures remained just as bright in this bleak place.

I rubbed my hands down my arms. The wind nipped at my exposed skin. Goose bumps rose on my arms. A jacket would have been nice right about now. The cold wasn't something I had anticipated. Who knew Hell wasn't all fire and brimstone? I unwrapped my shirt from around my nose and put it over my black top. At least my chest would be warm.

Fog trickled in the further I went. Without warning, the path sloped downwards. My feet skidded against rocks, stumbling at the sudden decline. One wrong step, and I'd tumble down to who knows what at the end of the slant. Cracked and broken stones scattered around the path ahead. The fog covered most of the land. The once evident path was now a misty white.

I let out a sigh as the path straightened out again. One less danger. Condensation clung to my clothes and hair. My breath mixed with the fog. I shivered. Pain raced up my legs. I paused, scanning my surroundings. I needed to rest, but where?

There had to be a better place than here. Red flashed passed me. I tensed, my hand on Lassemaica. Laughter filled the air. Chills ran down my spine. I knew that laugh, but it couldn't be. Tendrils of flaming red hair swirled in the mist.

"Aislin," a voice called, tinkling like bells.

My insides froze. I covered my ears. It wasn't real, she wasn't real, but she was. Emerald green eyes locked on to mine.

"Aislin Gray," she purred, "what a nice surprise."

My hand tightened on Lassemaica. The bow staff's weight comforted me. I'd defeat her like I had before. My eyes travelled around the path. Where the hell was she? The fog was so thick that I could barely make out my own feet. I gulped. Would she attack first? The hair on the back of my neck stood up.

"Poor, poor, Aislin, how's your dear Kaelin doing? Oh, right, I killed him." She chuckled, breath tickling the back of my neck.

I swung around. My staff struck empty air. She disappeared once more into the fog. I clenched my jaw. She had the upper hand. Seraphina was one of the three Court members who had sent me to the Abyss after I'd stood up for Kaydynce, demanding a fair trial, and the bitch who murdered Kaelin. She had drained him and left him for dead. Hell was turning out to be my worst nightmare.

Not only had I seen Aaron, but now I was about to face Seraphina once again. As if the first time hadn't been hard enough. She was quick as lightning with her enhanced senses and speed. Vampires were a pain in the ass to kill.

"Stop toying with me!"

"Oh, I've just begun. I'm going to enjoy killing you, since my last attempt wasn't effective enough. No matter. How's the stomach, by the way?" Pain ripped through my abdomen. I hunched forward, covering it with my arm. Warm liquid spread through my fingers. "Still tender, I see."

"Y-You bitch." I stumbled forward. The mist flickered in and out of my vision.

"Oh, hush now—no need to call each other names." Needle-like nails dug into my scalp. I cried out. She yanked my head back. I struggled.

The world spun. The pungent odor of copper drifted up my nose. Blood dripped onto the ground. My grip on my bow staff loosened. *Don't drop it. Please, don't drop it.*

"Mm, you smell delicious. I've waited a year for this. I should have drained you when I had the chance. The wait is over—I'll end you like I did your darling. He was quite sweet and intoxicating, I'll admit."

I blinked away the sudden drowsiness. Her voice drifted in and out. She was very talkative. My body went limp in her arms. Maybe if I pretended to give in, I'd catch her off guard. Vampires were susceptible once their prey gave in to their compulsion.

"Don't tell me you're giving up so easily? Where is the feisty banshee I've heard tales about? You know you're the talk of the Realm of the Dead. So many killed, all brought here."

Her breath was hot on my neck. Her tongue flicked across my pulse, leaving a warm trail of saliva. I shuddered.

Something sharp grazed against my skin. I flinched. Was that her nail or fangs? I couldn't tell. My heart thrashed against my rib cage. Fingers caressed down my arm, raising the hairs on my skin. I trembled.

"I-I don't know what you're talking about."

She chuckled. Soft lips nipped at my neck. My pulse jumped. This was worse than I had anticipated. Heat crept up my cheeks. Not only was she going to drain me, but she would make damn sure I enjoyed it. I needed to strike soon or else I would give in willingly.

"Don't act like you haven't killed anyone, little banshee," she whispered. Seraphina yanked my head back further. I winced.

"Just do it already!" I snapped. One bite then I could strike. Patience.

Black spots marred my vision. I gritted my teeth. The wound throbbed, blood leaking between my fingers. Goosebumps rose. My jaw twitched, teeth chattering.

"Patience is a virtue." She snickered, her breath searing on my exposed skin. The grip on my hair tightened. Strands of loose hair grazed my shoulder.

She traced a finger down the artery in my neck. Her nail sunk into my skin. I flinched.

"You bleed so easily." Seraphina's tongue lapped at the cut.

I didn't have time to register what was happening before pain and pressure hit me for a split second then pleasure. The pressure built, but it didn't hurt anymore. Heat coursed up my body.

"Ah, sweeter than I had anticipated," her voice echoed through my head, *"almost as sweet as your beloved Kaelin."*

I tensed. Now was my chance. Tightening my grip on my bow staff, I prepared to strike. Images flashed through my mind. I froze. Kaelin—the pictures were of Kaelin. The images were strung together to make a movie reel.

This wasn't happening. His death played in my head—courtesy of Seraphina. Through her eyes, I saw everything. Her slow saunter toward him, his trance-like face—golden eyes vacant, and the moment she sucked him dry. His mouthed words seared into my retinas. The words *I'm sorry* played on repeat.

My chest clenched. *Kaelin, I'm the one who should be sorry.* Tears burned a trail down my cheeks. I gulped, then jabbed backwards with as much force as I could muster. She cried out. My body flung forward. I crumbled to the ground, pain radiating through my stomach.

The Leaf Blade clattered to the dirt. Dark blood sizzled on one end of the energy blades. Despite the blades being made of energy, they still had the same effect as any other weapon.

Unlike heat energy that would cauterize a wound, their edges acted like real steel. I had found that out the hard way.

I scanned the fog. Was she gone? Silence filled the empty space surrounding me. The bite on my neck throbbed. Pain flickered on and off. I closed my eyes. I was a sitting duck, waiting to be picked off. Would she strike again?

I opened my eyes and fumbled for the Leaf Blade. If she attacked, I wanted to be ready. My fingers brushed the handle, but couldn't grasp it. The Leaf Blade reverted to its original form. The once double edged bow staff was now just a small stick with leaf designs etched into it.

A single drop of blood splashed to the ground. Colors peaked out from between the mist: blues, greens, golds, and sandy browns. Even the haze had a soft bluish hue. The colors lasted longer this time. Maybe it was the loss of blood, or maybe something else, but at that moment I felt peaceful. The calm before the storm. The chill in the air evaporated until I was numb. No pain and no cold.

"Little Miss Aislin, trying to save the world once more," the words hissed around me. I tensed. My fingers struggled to grip the blade. "I know why you're here. All of Hell knows," she whispered.

I swung backwards with my elbow. She hissed.

"This won't be the last time you see me, mark my words. Send Kaelin my regards, if you can find him." Her laughter echoed through the fog, fading with each passing second.

I slammed my fist against the ground. How dare she say his name. My shoulders slumped. Weariness overtook me. I blinked. Spots of color dotted my vision. The world spun even as I sat still. My eyelids drifted shut for a second, but that's all it took for everything to disappear.

~ ~ ~

"Is she dead?" a gravelly voice asked.

"Of course she is, why else would she be down here?" another replied.

"Who is she? Shouldn't there be a list or something for new arrivals?" the first asked.

"This isn't a hotel, it's not like we keep track—that's not our job, dipshit."

"Well, excuse me for wanting some sort of organizational system," the first huffed.

I blinked, groaning as I sat up.
"Oh! She's awake."

I squinted, assessing my surroundings. Seraphina. I tensed, heart pounding in my ears. Where was she? I whipped my body around, wincing at the pain in my stomach. The rocky path was nowhere in sight.

Icicles hung from the ceiling and the ground, protruding upwards from continuous water droplets. Mildew and muskiness invaded my nostrils. I wrinkled my nose. The walls were covered in ice. Underneath was a rocky surface. I could only assume I was in a cave. How had I gotten here?

"Jumpy little thing, isn't she?"

I turned toward the voice. Horns were the most prominent feature on his face. Sharp black and brown curved horns protruded from his forehead. He grinned. Mischief flashed in his dark eyes. Black, ragged wings hung comfortably on either side of his shoulder blades.

I froze.

Was this one of the demons I had prepared for? Remy hadn't known what I would face here. It was far from what I had expected. Something fluttered beside me. I scrambled backwards.

"See what I mean?" the horned one said.
"Will you just shut up, Azazel?"

"And who might this be?" A newcomer had entered the conversation.

The fluttering had been his wings—huge, golden wings. I gaped. The new arrival was bright compared to the other two, who were dark and brooding. Blonde hair fell past his ears, emphasizing his chiseled jawline. I couldn't help but stare. Silence crept in.

"We aren't sure yet. We found her yards from the abandoned houses—bleeding from an open wound on her abdomen."

The golden one's eyes narrowed. "So you decided to bring her here instead of leaving her there? Whose bright idea was that?"

The horned one, Azazel, fidgeted. The other one shook his head, dark hair shifting with the movement.

"It was Azazel's stupid idea. I told him to just leave her there. I told him it wasn't our place to interfere."

The newcomer glanced at Azazel and shook his head.

"Always the scapegoat. Well, since you two brought her here, it's only fair that you take her back."

I frowned. "Um, excuse me, but I'm right here—don't I get a say in this?"

All eyes landed on me. I gulped. Raised brows studied each little twitch as I twiddled my thumbs.

"Abaddon, drop the girl off where you found her, then report back here." Abaddon nodded and stepped forward.

I fumbled to my feet, wobbling for a moment. Pain stabbed up my stomach. I winced. My hands groped my jeans, searching. The Leaf Blade, where was it? I balled my hands into fists.

"Where is it?" Confusion passed across their faces. I exhaled. "You know damn well what I'm talking about. Now where is it?"

Azazel glanced at the other two then back at me. "Yeah, I have no idea what you're talking about. Um, maybe describe it for us?"

I closed my eyes and sucked in a breath then let it out slowly.

"Fine—my bow staff, that's what I'm looking for. It's a small stick that has leaves etched into it."

Blank faces stared back at me. I sucked in my lips. This was getting me nowhere. I threw my hands up in the air.

"You've got to be kidding me. None of you have seen an intricately-designed wooden staff? It's about yea big," I held up my hands about eight inches apart, "with squiggly leaves burned into the wood."

Seconds ticked by. Azazel's dark eyes lit up. His lips formed an O.

"Wait," he fished in his jean pocket, "is this it?" There in his hand was the Leaf Blade.

I stumbled toward him. Would it change forms for him too? His fingers wrapped around the handle as he held it out for me.

Before I even had the chance to grab for it, it morphed. The small staff extended a few more inches and curved inward. Red energy formed a straight line connecting both ends of the curve. The Leaf Blade had transformed into a bow. Silence followed suit.

Shit.

"What the fuck is that?" Abaddon pointed to the bow, glaring.

"Um, a hunting bow—obviously." Azazel plucked at the energy string. Another string of red energy appeared between the first string and the curved wood.

"I know that, dumbass. I'm talking about how it changed from a small stick to that."

"Will you two quiet down? Your bickering is giving me a headache." The golden one rubbed his fingers on either side of his temples.

"Um, I hate to interrupt, but can I have my staff back, please?"

All three glanced at each other. A hush fell over the room. I sighed. The golden one stepped toward me, wings extended. I stumbled backwards. If he was trying to look imposing, it worked.

"Where did you obtain such a weapon?"
I bit my lip. "It was thrust through my gut."

Azazel balked. "That's not how we found you. The staff was lying beside you."
I shook my head. "No, that's not what I meant. What I meant was it had been previously thrust into me before I got here."

"Is that how you died?"

"Azazel!" Abaddon punched his arm. "You can't just ask her something like that."

I frowned. "I'm not dead."
Abaddon and Azazel reeled back. "What?!?"

Chapter 10

"That's not possible. Nobody has entrance to Hell unless they're dead. Plain and simple."

"Says the dumbass who brought her here," Abaddon mumbled.

Azazel turned. His dark eyes smoldered. "What was that, Abaddon? Say it to my face, unless you're scared."

Abaddon's shoulders tensed. Wings I hadn't noticed before snapped open. Skin as thin as paper covered the expanse of his purple-black wings. Bat wings were more like it, except I could see individual feathers, almost transparent.

"I have no problem telling your dipshit face that you're the dumbass who brought a living being into our chambers." A deep rumble reverberated through the room. I shook. Azazel tackled Abaddon, slamming him against one of the ice-covered walls. Icicles shattered around them. I gasped. What the hell was happening? I watched, fear clutching my throat. Azazel lowered his head and rammed forward. Abaddon ducked. Azazel growled, struggling against the wall. His horns had penetrated the wall.

"Ha!" Abaddon shoulder-slammed into Azazel's gut, sending him flying.

Azazel skidded a few feet away. I fought the urge to run over to him. I didn't know this guy or demon or whatever he was, so why would I feel any emotion toward him? Weakness—that's what Illium would say. Shit. I needed to find Kaelin and Elijah and get the hell out of here. How though?

The Leaf Blade—that was my ticket home. I glanced at Azazel. His hands were empty.

He picked himself back up and charged, his head bowed. I squeezed my eyes shut. I waited for the bone-shattering impact, or at least the sound, but it never came.

"Will you two try to act civil?"

I opened one eye, then the other as the danger had passed. The golden one stood with hands stretched outwards between the other two. His white-gold wings were ruffled. Tension crackled in the icy room. Nobody dared to move.

"You're more bull-headed than Lord of Goats. Though I suppose goats have the same attributes, but I digress." Golden eyes locked onto me. I fidgeted under his intense gaze. "We must deal with the matter at hand." I didn't like the sound of that.

"Now then, how is it a living being was able to pass through the threshold of Hell? It doesn't happen by accident. So, tell me, miss," he paused. "What's your name, dear?"

I shuffled my feet. Stop that! I straightened. There was no reason to be ashamed of who I was. I took a deep breath.

"Aislin Gray."

Everyone froze. Abaddon was the first to break the ice.

"Ah, fuck. That's her?"

The golden one sighed. "Just as I suspected. I heard rumors of a living and not just any—Aislin Gray, the one who released everything in Abaddon's own creation—the
Abyss."

"Oh no, no, no, no, shit—I didn't know, Belial, you have to believe me."

The one called Belial sucked in a breath then smiled. "I'll deal with you later, but right now Lucifer needs to be notified about the breech if he doesn't already know."

Azazel nodded. He bolted through the only opening I could see and disappeared. This was it—my end. I gulped.

"What now, Belial?" Abaddon asked, glancing from Belial to me then back again.

"We wait for Azazel to return then go from there—that's all we can do for now."

I let out the breath I had been holding. I wasn't going to die or at least not yet. I shook my head. What kind of thinking was that? Fight or flight, though apparently, there wasn't a flight option, just a giving up one. Damn it, this wasn't helping. Escape route.

First, I needed my weapon back. Azazel had dropped it before his fight with Abaddon, but where? I scanned the icy room. There! A few feet away was the Leaf Blade. The problem—getting past Belial. It was inches away from the tip of Belial's left wing.

Speed would be my advantage, or maybe surprise. Either way I was getting my staff back. With Azazel gone and both Abaddon and Belial distracted, I went for it. I had a split second to change my mind, but there was no going back. I ran toward my staff and slid under Belial's wing. Both turned, but by that point the Leaf Blade was back in my hands. The moment it touched my palm, it changed. Abaddon stared, wide eyed.

Belial frowned. "What do you think you are doing?"

I stood up, bow staff at the ready. "I'm getting the hell out of here, and you can't stop me."

The corner of Belial's lips lifted. He waved his hands in a wide arc. "Go right ahead."

"What the fuck, man? I thought you didn't want her to leave," Abaddon whispered, glancing at my bow staff.

Belial moved his head slowly toward Abaddon. He quieted down immediately. I narrowed my eyes. What was he planning? I tightened my grip on my staff and side-stepped them. I kept an eye focused on them. My hands itched for a fight. Belial held up his hands, palms open before taking a step forward. I tensed. He paused. The corners of his lips turned up a little bit more.

"Don't worry, I'm not trying to stop you. But this is a dangerous place for a beautiful girl such as yourself. I'd hate to see harm come to you, if there was a way I could have prevented it."

I rolled my eyes and swung my bow staff around with the flick of my wrist.

"I think I can handle myself just fine, thank you very much."

He bowed. "Very well, but don't say I didn't warn you."

I squared my shoulders. I'd faced many dangers already, what was a little bit more? Show no fear. He didn't scare me. I strode through the opening with head held high. The contrast of dark to light burned my retinas. I shielded my eyes.

The other room had ice covering the walls, but it was nothing compared to the shimmering blocks of ice and light fragments that reflected at me. I rubbed my arms. My breath fogged in front of me. While the other room had been cave-like, this was an open space. Squinting, I looked around. Nothing out of the ordinary unless a frozen world counted.

The fissured ceiling vanished, in its place—ice. Light refracted, bouncing off the crystalized water. Rainbows were everywhere—blinding colors of reds, oranges, yellows, greens, blues, and purples. I stood in awe.

Who knew ice could be beautiful? I walked further out into the icy expanse, taking it all in. No more fire and brimstone. I was close to the core. A snap echoed off the ice. I tensed, tightening my grip on the Leaf Blade. All Hell broke loose.

More snaps reverberated through the place. A chunk of ice toppled in front of me. I jumped back. The ground shook. I stumbled forward. Something cracked under me. I grimaced. I didn't have to look down to know the ice splintered open underneath my legs. The fissure broke off into smaller cracks. The ground broke around me. I searched for another way out. I wasn't about to fall through a gap in the ice.

Push forward or turn back—those were my options. Give in and turn into a coward who couldn't do anything by herself or be strong and defy the odds? There was no choice. Taking a deep breath, I pressed on. The cracks weren't wide enough to fall through yet, but spraining my ankle was a high possibility. The ice-scape went on as far as my eyes could see. Was this the bottom of Hell? I shook my head. No, this didn't seem right. The fractures, forgotten for the moment, burst.

Cackles and chattering filled the ice-scape. Shit. Tiny black bodies swarmed from the gaps in the ice. Thousands of red, beady eyes glared at me. Small black bat wings protruded from their shoulders. Demons, or at least the demons I'd expected to encounter.

My grip tightened on my bow staff. I itched for a fight. There was no room for doubt. Thousands of bodies clambered toward me. I stood my ground, one leg forward and knees bent. All the training I had done was for this moment—to fight. The first wave of demons buckled forward, kicking and clawing at each other.

I grinned. Easy as pie. I swung my staff downwards then upwards, flinging demons left and right. They kept coming. The twenty I killed, twenty more appeared. A never-ending battle. They pushed forward. I pushed back. Black blood coated the ice. I was losing ground though—more popped up. Too many. My heart raced.

The chilly air stung my lungs with each ragged breath I took. Small scratches covered my arms from where some had snuck in a hit. I wasn't giving up. I pushed onward despite my back being against the wall. One of me and who knew how many of them.

The demons flooded out of the crevasses like a black river. I slipped and stumbled as more blood was spilt. I ground my teeth. My muscles ached. With each swing of my bow staff, the more my body cried out. Sweat dripped down my brow. I blew it away.

I couldn't afford to be distracted. Any mistake could cost me my life. I scanned the ice-scape, searching for something: be it an escape route or something to use against them— anything would work. A grin spread across my face. A few feet away was a cracked glacier. If I cracked it more, then it'd crash onto the ice and hopefully take out some demons.

All I needed was to get a little bit closer. I backed up further. The black mass of demons followed my movements. A little bit more. My back slammed into a wall of ice. Damn it. I glanced up. The icy rock hung over top of me. One slice and it would break. That's all I had to do, just swing my bow staff and it would come crashing down.

Tightening my grip on the Leaf Blade, I swung with all the strength I could muster. The energy blade sliced through the ice like butter. The glacier catapulted down, smashing demons into the ice. I sighed, crumbling to the ground. It wasn't over yet.

More demons skidded and jumped over the ice slab. Snickers and hisses echoed off the walls. I had to get up. I struggled back on my feet, the bow staff supporting some of my weight. I needed a plan. *Think, Aislin, think.* I racked my brain for something—anything that I could use to defeat them.

Nothing.

My muscles screamed for relief. Thousands of unblinking, beady eyes stared. None moved any closer. If anything, they backed up. A small path opened, leading back the way I came. I shook my head. There was no way I was going backwards. I stood my ground. Kaelin needed me, Elijah needed me—I wasn't leaving, not yet.

"Stubborn, I see. Lucifer may have use of you."

I glared at the approaching form. Belial, the golden one, stood in the middle of the river of demons. He smirked.

Golden wings fluttered slightly before settling back against his shoulder blades.

"I hope this isn't a bad time."

"Nope. Just killing demons—you know, nothing special."

Belial grinned, showing off his pearly whites. "Looked more like they were hurting you more than you were hurting them."

I crossed my arms over my chest, body groaning with the movement. The Leaf Blade hung by my side.

"I had it under control," I shuffled my feet, "but I guess I should thank you."

He bowed, hand over his heart. "No thanks are needed," he glanced up through his eyelashes, "but to be honest, you did better than I anticipated. So it is I whom should be thanking you for exceeding my expectations."

My brow furrowed, eyes scrunching closer together. "Hold on, are you saying this was your doing—sending demons to kill me?"

Belial straightened and shrugged. "Kill is such a strong word. I prefer maimed, mutilated, weakened even. Death does not apply."

"So, what? Why try to *maim* me? You said I could leave—didn't take you long to change your mind."

"Forgive me, but I do love a good fight. Blood and gore—burning rage that comes with war," he gestured at the thousands of demons and the blood-soaked ice, "I relish in human nature—lust and pride, both worthy of rapture. I'm also a bit of a liar—did I forget to say that? I'm not called Lord of Lies for nothing."

"What now? Am I supposed to just give in? Bow down to you, like some god? You can go fuck yourself if that's the case."

Belial's grin widened. He held out his index finger and stroked it with his other index. "Tsk tsk, what foul language. Giving in is so boring." His eyes lit up. "Now, putting up a fight, that's more like it."

I tensed. I unraveled my arms and tightened my grip on the Leaf Blade. If a fight was what he wanted, then a fight he would get. There was no backing down. I only had a split second to decide my answer before he flew at me. I ducked, tumbling away. I crouched, staff at the ready. He struck once more, wings extended. I dodged, summersaulting a few feet away. Laughter filled the ice-scape, echoing off the walls.

"Isn't this fun!"

Fun was not the word I would use. Being chased by a man with wings was not my idea of a good time. Running wasn't an option. It was either fight or die trying. I straightened, knees still bent, and prepared for the next assault. It didn't take long. Belial circled back around then landed a few feet away. His wings folded against his back.

"Come now, where is the fight, the drive to stay alive? That survival instinct most humans have—though I suppose you aren't truly human. But none the less, it's still there. Let it out—be free."

I wanted to laugh. Be free? How could I ever be free if I was being chased down by a demon with bird wings, had to finish a deal I made with an elf, and find Kaelin's soul before I even thought about leaving this hellhole?

I shook my head. Freedom was a luxury I didn't have. Lucifer. I slammed my palm against my forehead. Dumbass. Elijah was in Lucifer's chambers. The answer had been staring me in the face the whole time. I lowered the Leaf Blade. Belial raised a brow.

"I give up. Take me to Lucifer." *Take me to Elijah.*

Belial's lower lip puckered out a bit. His eyes twinkled with mirth. "Awe, too bad. I would have loved for a bit more cat and mouse, but very well."

He strode over, confidence rolled off him in waves. A grin spread across his lips. I stiffened, unsure of what to expect. My heart pounded in my ears. He wrapped an arm around my waist and pulled me close. His wings snapped open.

He leaned in closer. "Hold on tight, Aislin Gray." His breath tickled my ear.

Chapter 11

Aislin

Being held by a demon (or whatever he was) was not on my to-do list, even though he was handsome. If it got me to Lucifer, then I'd do what I had to. Belial's arms held me tight against his chest. The takeoff was jarring. He ran a few feet before his wings snapped open, catching the current. We were thrust into the air. I clung to him. We glided through the pale sky. Occasionally his wings would flap, lifting us higher. Despite the circumstances, the ice-scape held a beauty that could only be appreciated from above.

The rainbows the light refracted glittered as the tips of Belial's wings sliced through them. I was awestruck.

"It's magnificent, is it not?" His voice carried on the wind.

I kept quiet. There was no point in making small talk. I had a job to do, and I intended to do just that. Being friendly to a demon was not one of the criteria.

"Ah, I see. The silent treatment—how appropriate. Very well then."

The rest of the flight stayed that way. I didn't talk, and he stopped trying. The ice-scape went on for miles. Glacier after glacier, with nothing in-between. I must have dozed off at one point. The next thing I knew, we were falling. I opened my mouth to scream, but no sound came out. My heart jumped to my throat. The ice-scape rushed toward us. I tightened my grip on his back and the Leaf Blade. Belial's wings were tucked, propelling us downward.

"Don't strangle me," he chuckled.

His wings snapped open. The force of the wind caught his feathers, lifting us up. We glided back down again. The minute my feet touched the ground, I let go.

"Sorry," I mumbled.
He grinned. "No apology needed."

I nodded, surveying the new landscape. Stairs led down to where we were. That explained the sudden falling sensation—steep stairs. I shivered. The temperature had dropped a few more degrees.

"Aislin Gray, welcome. I've been expecting you."

I followed the voice to the back of the cave-like room. A round staircase led up to an ice throne. There on the top step stood a man. No words could do him justice. I thought Belial had the devilishly good looks, but there was no comparison.

Pure white wings rested against his back. Belial was bright, but Lucifer shone like a star. I stumbled forward. Long blonde hair fell right below his shoulders. This was the devil. My pulse skyrocketed. *Focus*. I took a deep breath and searched the place for the reason I was here—Elijah.

Two doors remained closed on either side of the throne. Was Elijah in there? There was no way of knowing. Wouldn't he keep his Hell hounds close, and where were Abaddon and Azazel?

"Are you just going to stand there, all flustered? Don't get me wrong, it's kind of cute, but Lucifer is a busy man and doesn't like waiting."

I jumped. I had forgotten Belial was beside me.
"I'm not flustered," I grumbled, shaking his words off.
This was the devil after all. Scared, yes—flustered, no.

The corners of Belial's lips lifted.

"Then go ahead." He pushed me forward.

I tripped over my feet. I turned and glared at Belial. Just walk toward the devil—easy, said no one ever. Lucifer stood poised and regal on top of his throne. Shoulders back, head held high—confidence, the one thing I need right about now. With posture in mind, I strode up to Lucifer. What next? I hadn't thought any of this through. Panic settled in. I bit my lip.

Lucifer smiled and bowed. "I've heard many of tales about you and your quest."

I gulped. "Q-Quest?"

His smile widened. "Yes. I have eyes and ears everywhere. Sadly, I must inform you of how vain it is. You see, unlike my followers—Belial, Abaddon, and Azazel—I keep track of all who enter my realm." My chest dropped. I knew where this was going. "Your lover isn't here."

I shook my head. He had to be here. My hands shook. "N-No, he's here—he has to be here. You didn't know I was here, so how do you know he isn't here too?"

Lucifer sighed. "I know everything that happens here—the minute you fell through Hell, your encounter with both Aaron and Seraphina, and your fight with Belial's demons, which was impressive, I might add."

"I don't believe you."

He nodded. "Believe what you like, but that's the truth.

Now on to the other reason why you are here."

I stiffened. My fingers tensed on the Leaf Blade. Lucifer's blue eyes danced.

"Elijah!" he called, whistling once.

The door to the right opened. A wolf as tall as Lucifer strutted out. It had sandy brown fur with white tufts on its paws.

Holy shit!

He was massive. How the hell was I supposed to get him out of here? Damn it, Illium. Nothing was going as planned. Elijah stalked closer with hackles raised and canines exposed. His breath frosted in the air. A deep growl emanated from his body. The ice shook under my feet. He was the epitome of the big, bad wolf. I might as well be one of the three little pigs hiding in a house.

"Why don't you say hello to our new guest, Elijah?"

The hair on the back of my neck stood up. His nostrils flared as he turned. Big hazel eyes focused on me. My heart pounded in my ears. Would he attack me? The Leaf Blade slipped between my fingers and clattered to the icy floor.

The wolf's head tilted and its ears perked up. Belial chuckled behind me. Heat raced up my cheeks. Show no fear—ha—too late. I gulped. This wolf could crush me if he wanted to. I bent down and reached for the Leaf Blade. His eyes followed my every movement. Silence trickled in. The only thing that could be heard were our breaths.

Elijah stepped closer, nails scraping on the ice. I cringed. Chills ran up and down my spine. His ears flattened against his skull, and his underbelly touched the floor. A whine pierced the silence, high and eerie. Lucifer grinned, walking down the stairs.

"Intimidating, isn't he? One of the best Hell hounds I've found. It would be a shame to lose him. Now if there was an equal trade, then I'd gladly let him go."

One of Elijah's ears lifted. I bit my lip. A trade? What could the devil possibly want from me?

"What do you want?" Was I about to make a deal with the devil?

Lucifer's grin widened. He stopped beside Elijah, putting a hand on his scruff. The wolf's body shook under his touch. At least I wasn't the only one afraid of what was about to happen. No good could come of it.

"Oh, nothing too drastic. Don't worry, I'm not asking for your soul—that's too cliché. I am, however, willing to trade my dear Elijah for Illium Dreamer."

"W-What?" There had to be a catch. "All you want is Illium's soul? That's it, nothing else?"

Lucifer nodded. "Yes. Do we have a deal?"

I shook my head. "Say I took the deal, how am I supposed to get his soul? It's not like there is a machine for that or something."

Lucifer laughed and spread out his arms. White wings opened, spanning the length of his arms.

"How else? You kill him."
I held up my hands "Woah, I can't just kill him."

He shrugged. "It's not hard. It wouldn't be your first time. From what I've been told, you've killed many supernatural creatures."

"T-that's not the same."

He raised a brow. "Isn't it though? From the stories that I've heard, you've killed quite a few beings that you, yourself, released from The Abyss."
I fidgeted. "I-I only killed the ones who were murdering innocent people."
The corners of his lips curved upwards. He shook his index finger. "Ah and there's the kicker—who's to say who is innocent and who is not? One person may think another is innocent and not know that person is a killer.

"Everyone sins. Nobody is innocent. Someone considered a terrorist is a hero somewhere else." He studied me then bowed his head. "Ah, still not convinced I see. How about I sweeten the deal? If your man happens to show up here, I'll let you know."

That wasn't something I could take lightly. If I said yes, I'd be killing someone I know. It was one thing to kill a murderer, but it was completely different with Illium. I mean, sure, he wasn't my friend or anything, but I still wouldn't want to kill him, despite him being a complete ass at times.

I sighed. "No." I couldn't do it.

Lucifer frowned, arms falling to his sides. "Well that's disappointing. I suppose I should have expected it. Are you sure I can't persuade you?"

I shook my head. "Pity. Belial!" he called.

Wings whooshed behind me. I turned. Belial's arms wrapped around my torso, pinning my arms to my sides. I struggled. The Leaf Blade hung limp in my hand. His wings created a cocoon. The under plumes tickled my face.

"Stop squirming, you're only going to hurt yourself," Belial whispered.

I kicked and thrashed more. There was no way I was about to give up after everything I had been through just to get here.

"Let me go," I growled.

He laughed. "And lose my wings? I think not. No one disobeys Lucifer."

Think, Aislin, think. "Please, you're hurting me," I whimpered.

His grip tightened. I winced. He leaned closer, his breath hot on my neck.

"Lucifer will do much worse if I let you go." I stilled. "That's better."

"Belial, bring Aislin to me, I'd like to show her something."

My feet lifted off the ground as Belial strode over to him.

"Set her down here, keep a good grip on her. Wouldn't want her to get loose now, would we?"

"No, sir." Belial's wings fell open, resting against his back once more.

"Good, now then," Lucifer's fingers caressed Elijah's neck. The wolf shook. His hand grasped then yanked something from Elijah's neck. The wolf yelped, flinging his head toward Lucifer. A large, metal collar clattered to the icy floor.

"Now watch." Lucifer's blue eyes danced. He clasped his hands together.

Right before my eyes, the wolf shrunk. The long, sandy brown fur receded, exposing tan skin. Where his huge paws had been, hands appeared. Both his ears and tail disappeared. My mouth fell open. There in front of me was a naked man. He laid in the fetal position, head tucked under his arms.

"H-How did you," I struggled with the words, "h-how, I-I thought—change at will?" If I could slap myself, I would. Incoherent words.

Lucifer chuckled. "Normally, a werewolf can change forms, depending on when he/she was bit. Human folklore got some things correct. The ones bit on a full moon turn during one, while some are born."

What the hell? I was getting useful information from the devil—the last person I ever imagined. Elijah lifted his head and glared.

"Thanks. I just loved wearing that thing."

Lucifer grinned. "If you behave, you won't have to wear it ever again."

Elijah sat up on his knees. "Really? Oh boy, oh boy." Sarcasm dripped off his words. "Yeah, I doubt that." He turned to me with a raised brow. "Now, are we going or what?"

I gulped. Lucifer's grin faltered. "I think not. It would be wise of you to hold your tongue, beast."

Elijah's lips curved into a lopsided grin. "Or else what? You can't do anything to me. I'm already dead."

Shit. Pure white wings snapped open. Lucifer rose above him. The ice room darkened, turning an ominous blue. I shivered. Lucifer's shadow lengthened.

"On the contrary, I can. This is my domain—what I say goes. I could have let you suffer in one of the torture rooms, but instead I allowed you to be one of my Hell Hounds. I won't make that mistake again." Lucifer snapped his fingers. The ice cracked.

Demons spewed out of the chasm. Black masses flooded the ice room. Thousands of red, beady eyes waited for their next order. Snickers and sneers echoed off the walls.

"Now you've done it, hound. Let's hope it's only you he teaches a lesson to," Belial spat. Could this get any worse?

Lucifer spread his arms out wide. "Come my children, feast your eyes on your next meal—the tortured soul of a werewolf." All eyes landed on Elijah. He tensed.

Some of the demons licked their lips, while others bared tiny, razor-sharp teeth. Chaos ensued. Demons flew toward him. A scream ripped from my throat.

I wasn't about to watch another person die—not like this. I'm not quite sure how, but when I screamed, Belial and I were flung backwards. His wings stopped our momentum. The demons scattered, withering and crying out. No one said a word.

Lucifer raised a brow and clapped. "Quite a show, Miss Aislin. I would have never fathomed such a thing was possible if I hadn't seen it with my own eyes. Well done."

I frowned. "I don't know what you're talking about."

He chuckled, shaking his head. "Ah, ignorant. Shall we test it again?" He nodded. "Take her away."

"Yes, sir."

Belial's arms tightened. I thrashed. His grip never faltered, not even once. My blood boiled. Damn him, damn them all. I ground my teeth and twisted my wrist. If I could just swing the Leaf Blade and catch him off guard, then I could free myself. Unlikely though.

"Let me go."
"Not a chance, sweetheart."
I clenched my jaw. "Let. Me. Go."

Belial chuckled. "Nope."

My vision clouded. "LET ME GO!" I screamed.

Ice shattered. The throne splintered and cracked down the middle. Belial and I were sent backwards. He skidded, falling to one knee. His hands loosened. I sprung away, taking a defensive stance. I wasn't sure what had happened, but there was no time to think. I jumped into action. I swung the Leaf Blade, spinning it in my hands. No one moved. Lucifer grinned, eyes glinting. The scream barely affected him.

He glided down. His wings settled against his back. I tensed. What was he planning? I glanced at Elijah. He hadn't moved an inch. Lucifer raised his arms and spread them out. The demons that were left lifted their heads and fluttered their wings. A split second, that was all I had.

"Run!" The demons swarmed.

I dashed forward, bow staff slicing through demons left and right. A deep growl emanated from Elijah. The walls shook. Demons were flung through the air. The wolf was back. I gulped. That was a good thing, right? Blood coated the floor. I had to get to Elijah. More demons sprouted from the crevasse. Shit. I spun and kicked my way to him.

"We need to get out of here." I placed a hand on his shoulder. He reared back and swiped. Air whooshed passed my face. A nail grazed my cheek. I winced but held strong. The demons circled. Their beady eyes followed our every move.

Shit, shit, shit.

My grip tightened on the Leaf Blade. I took a deep breath. *Please let this work.* I raised the Leaf Blade over my head before slamming it down into the ice. Nothing happened. Damn it! I raised it again, praying for it to work.

A hole opened, blinding light shining through. The hole widened. The light swirled in a vortex of white.

"Jump!" Some of the demons clawed and swatted at our clothes. Elijah jumped first, passing through easily. I jumped.

"Leaving so soon?" Wings whipped behind me. An arm wrapped around my midriff. "Don't worry. This won't take long."

Chills ran up and down my spine. The portal shrunk in size. I struggled. I had to get through, or else I'd be stuck here forever. Lucifer chuckled.

"Remember what I asked for," he whispered before letting go. I screamed.

Voices drifted through the vortex. My screams quieted, throat scratchy.

"Where is she?"
"She was right behind me."

An opening appeared seconds later. I was spit out. I crashed to the floor. I sucked in a breath, wincing. Pain radiated through my spin.

"Aislin, thank God! I thought I was going to have to rescue you."

I smiled, picking myself up and brushing off my pants. "I appreciate the gesture, but I made it back. Just a few cuts and bruises."

Remy chuckled. "I can see that. You're a mess."

I rolled my eyes. "I'm just glad I'm back in the real world." Kaelin wasn't though. My shoulders slumped.

Remy rested a hand on my shoulder. "We will find him." I frowned. He pushed his glasses up. "Elijah told me."

I nodded. Of course. Elijah shrugged. "Didn't think it was a secret."

I sighed. "It's fine. Anyways, I'm going to lie down."

I shuffled to the mattress in the corner of the training room. My muscles groaned as I curled up under my blanket.

It was finally over.

Chapter 12

Kaydynce

"The time has come, my queen."

I straightened, heart racing. This was really happening. "Really? You found him?"

Illium chuckled, resting a finger against my lips. "Not quite, but soon. Your friend, Aislin, has returned from the Realm of the Dead."

I crossed my arms over my chest. "She's not my friend. I despise her."

The corners of Illium's lips lifted, indigo eyes shining. "Such hatred, I love it."

I giggled, nipping his finger. He growled. His arms snaked around my waist and yanked me against him. I ran a hand down his chest.

"So . . . is there a reason why you have been waiting for her return? Don't tell me it's because you want her instead of me." I pouted.

He ran his thumb down my jutted-out lip before pinching my chin. His eyes danced. "Never. You are the stars above, twinkling like a thousand diamonds. Whereas she is merely a bottom-feeding oyster."

I clapped my hands together. "No, no, she is like a cockroach under our feet."

Illium smirked, leaning in close. "Eloquently said, my love." His lips brushed mine before he took a step back. "Now then, I must be off. My reacquired soul awaits."

My eyes narrowed, lips tightening. "Let me guess, you have to go see her."

Illium shook his index finger. "Tsk, tsk, my sweet. Jealousy does not become you."

I pouted, crossing my arms over my chest. "Can I at least accompany you?"

He sighed. "Alas, you cannot. You are needed here, to protect our kingdom from unwanted guests."

"B-But, why can't the guards do that? Isn't that their job? I'll behave, I swear!"

Illium shook his head. White blonde hair shifted with his movements. "My queen needs to stay in the kingdom where the guards can do their job as I have ordered. Don't forget, time works differently here."

I rolled my eyes. "You've said that, but what does that even mean?"

He sighed and rested a hand on my cheek. Chills ran across my skin. "Time here is only a fraction of the human realm. Which means a year here is close to two years over there. Your body would catch up to you in that time frame."

"Um, so? You act like I would care about something like that. I mean, sure, I love my looks, but a year is nothing—now if it was five or ten years, then we would have a problem."

He closed his eyes for a second. "Kaydynce." I stiffened at the use of my name. "Stay here, with your guards. I won't be long."

I nodded, my shoulders slumping. He smiled and patted my cheek. Illium raised a hand. A bluish light burst from nothing, outlining a doorway. Without a second glance at me, he walked through. I tapped my fingers on my arm. Should I?

My feet itched to go through the doorway with him. The archway thinned, the light dimming. There was no point in thinking about it, I knew what I wanted. I ran through the portal. It snapped close behind me.

Darkness shrouded me. The air hummed. The hairs on the back of my neck stood on end. My heart thumped against my chest, echoing in my ears. Deep breaths, I'd seen Illium do it a thousand times. Piece of cake. My legs trembled as I walked into the darkness.

"Think of where you want to go, and you will be there," Illium's voice echoed in my head.

I closed my eyes. Where did I want to go? A doorway opened in front of me. With shaky hands, I pushed open the door. The black of night greeted me.

Crickets chirped their incessant songs. The second my feet touched the pavement, the portal disappeared. I glanced at my surroundings. Houses lined the road. I knew this neighborhood. Images of playing hop-scotch on the sidewalk and skipping rope with Aislin flashed through my mind.

I glanced down the street to my right, and there it was—Aislin's house, the house at the end of the road. Too many memories, both happy and painful, were associated with that place. I clenched my jaw. Why had the doorway led me here?

Of all the places I wanted to go, this was not one of them. I shook head. There was no turning back now, even if I could. *Damn you, Aislin.* No matter what I did, she was there—always interfering. Taking a deep breath, I pressed onward. At least I could see my grandma.

I hung my head, my shoulders slumping. Was she worried about me? No, if anything she'd scold me for disappearing, in true grandma fashion. Maybe I wouldn't see her.

Street lamps flickered soft lights, illuminating my path. The night air nipped at my exposed skin. I rubbed my hands over my arms. When had it gotten so cold? A gust of wind whipped strands of hair into my eyes. I brushed it aside.

The noise of the night stopped. I froze. I tilted my head to the side and waited. Nothing happened. Odd, even the damn crickets were silent. Rocks skipped and skidded under my feet as I walked on.

Darkness hovered—a cat anticipating to pounce. House after house passed by. What time was it? I glanced at the sky. Stars twinkled, but the moon was nowhere to be found. I shrugged. Not like I knew astronomy anyways.

I meandered without a destination in mind. I breathed in the night air. The corners of my lips lifted. This was nice. The Other Realm was nice too, but there was something about being back in the Human Realm that was better. Home, that's what it was—that's why I'd craved the Human Realm.

I frowned, shaking my head. No, that was absurd—how could I crave something I'd never had? Sure, I'd had a roof over my head, but I wouldn't consider it a home. If the saying was true: home is where the heart is, then I'd had no home or heart for that matter. Love required a heart, and I sure as Hell never loved anyone other than myself.

Thoughts of Illium fluttered through my head. The feel of his icy skin under my fingertips, the taste of his lips—along with his life-force, and the way his indigo eyes darkened or brightened, depending on his mood. He was different.

I closed my eyes. The corners of my lips lifted for a moment then faltered. Violet—if he knew I had left, that's the color his eyes would be. Shit. I took a deep breath. Maybe he wouldn't be that mad. Ha! Of course he would be. Chills ran up and down my arms. The cold was nothing compared to what Illium would cause.

I shook it off, holding my head up high. I was his queen. He wouldn't dare do anything. My strides quickened. The street lights dimmed. The darkness surrounding me moved closer, its claws digging into my arms. The world wasn't so nice anymore.

Click, click, click.

My heels picked up tempo, matching my pulse. Why was I here? I second guessed my decision. Memory lane was not what I wanted. *Impulsive* is what Aislin would say. I ground my teeth. Aislin—the slut who'd destroyed everything. Why couldn't she have died instead of Kaelin? We all would have been better off anyways.

He was mine, then little miss sunshine had gotten in the way. She was the reason he had left in the first place, but then he came back. He had come back for me. I licked my lips. *Kaelin, soon we will be together again*. He would be mine again, and Aislin would be out of the picture.

A smirk played across my lips. Soon. Soon it would be her turn. Until then, I had to wait. Patience was not something I liked, but the anticipation of her inevitable death would make it all the sweeter. With that in mind, I walked.

Excitement bubbled. Images of all the ways she could die filtered through my head. Hopefully slow. The more I walked and thought, the stronger my strides became. Fear left and eagerness took its place.

A slow, painful death. A girl could dream. I sighed, imagining her face: blue eyes wide, skin even paler, and perfect lips parted as blood gushed and pooled. A cry scattered my thoughts. My eyes narrowed as I pursed my lips.

How dare they? I stormed toward the noise. Sobs echoed through the night. Pain followed the sound. I breathed it in, reveling in it. A gnawing ache clenched my stomach. I licked my lips. Hunger fueled me forward.

My eyes locked on to my prey. I crept closer. She laid on the street, crumpled in a heap. Her cries intensified, her body racked with pain. My mouth watered.

"Why so sad?" I asked, voice low and soft. No reason to cause any more fear than needed.

Her head whipped around, red-brown hair flying. I froze. Wide, crystal blue eyes stared. Her pale skin was pink and blotchy from her tears. I gulped. My pulse and hers pounded in my ears.

"K-Kaydynce?" Her voice shook.
Silence.

She scrambled up and wiped her face. My grin widened as I nodded. This was perfect. I couldn't have asked for a better opportunity. More tears fell as she ran to me. Her arms wrapped around my neck.

"Oh, Kay, I was so worried about you. After we escaped the Court, you vanished. I wasn't sure what happened to you."

"Shh." I placed her head on my shoulder despite being a couple inches shorter. "I'm safe. Illium has been taking care of me."

She stiffened, pulling back. "Illium? Um, t-that's good, as long as you're doing well." A look crossed her face then it was gone.

I chuckled. It was no surprise how she felt about Illium.

All the things I could tell her—the battle of the Other Realm, how I became a queen, but why would I let her spoil everything again? "Never been better."

Aislin nodded, sniffling. "Um, I-I guess you've already heard."

Heard what? I frowned, racking my brain then it dawned on me. My shoulders slumped. Kaelin. I sucked in a breath. *Choose your words carefully, Kaydynce.* Patience was key.

I cast my eyes down. "Yeah ... I can't believe it's been a year now."

"It haunts my every waking moment . . . and my dreams," she choked out.

It had fucking better. You let him die! I held my tongue. She'd get what she deserved in due time.

"Time heals all wounds." Blah, blah, blah, and that other bullshit.

More tears trickled down her cheeks. "I-I tried to bring him back, but h-he wasn't there. I don't know what else to do, Kaydynce. My head knows he's gone, but my heart says otherwise." She glanced back at where she had been. "I came here hoping to hear his voice again, to see his face just one more time, but all I see is him dying—letting go of his last breath."

I clenched my fists. What a bitch! My legs shook as I stepped toward her. This was where *my* Kaelin had died—where she'd *let* him die. I couldn't hold it back any longer.

Anger swirled and embraced me. "H-How could you?"

Her brows furrowed. "What?"

"How could you!" I repeated, venom dripping from my words.

She reared back, mouth falling open. "I don't understand. How could I do what?"

I pursed my lips. "And I thought I was the ditz. How the fuck could you have let him die? I thought saving people was your thing, but apparently not. Or maybe you didn't love him as much as you said you did. Either way you let him die, and I will never forgive you!"

Aislin's eyes widened. She stumbled backwards, tripping over her feet. She fell, her ass hitting the asphalt.

"K-Kaydynce, it wasn't like that. I-I tried to save him, but I was too late."

"Liar!" I yelled. "You let him die!"

She shook her head. "Please, Kay, just listen . . ."

"Don't call me that!" Energy snaked and withered around me. "I don't want to hear any more of your lies!" I stalked closer.

Her heart pounded in my ears. Waves of fear hit my nose. I grinned, breathing it in. She shuffled away, scrambling to her feet. "Kay, I mean, Kaydynce, don't do this."

I raised a brow. "Don't do what exactly, Aislin? Don't get revenge for killing Kaelin? Don't kill you? I suppose they're the same thing," I shrugged, "but I'll enjoy every second of watching you wither in pain and pleasure."

Her hand fumbled for something at her waist. I closed the gap, reaching for Aislin's throat. She jumped back. I lunged forward. My fingers grazed her leg as she summersaulted to the right. Aislin picked herself up and took a fighting stance. "I don't want to hurt you."

"The funny thing is that I do—want to hurt you, that is." She stood her ground. I licked my lips.

"Then you leave me no choice," she said.

Aislin grasped a small hilt. In a blink of an eye, it extended to the length of her body. The white blades on either side pulsed in the darkness.

"Nice weapon, but I doubt you'll actually use it on me. We are friends after all, right? You wouldn't hurt a friend— oh wait, you did. You killed him the moment he came back. How does that make you feel, knowing you were the reason why he died? His death is on your hands. I bet you didn't even try to save him—coward."

Aislin's grip tightened on the bow staff. My grin widened. *Yes, get angry—let me feel your hatred and hurt.* Strong emotions were more filling than subtle hints. Tears streamed down her face. She screamed and charged, staff raised. I laughed and dodged. Aislin swung back around with the other side. I ducked.

I puckered my lips. "Aw, did I hit a nerve? If I killed you here, that would be poetic, right? Two lovers dying in the same spot, a year apart. SOOO romantic."

"Stop this, Kaydynce. This is no place for a fight. If you cared about Kaelin at all then let this be his resting place, nothing more."

I shook my head. "Nice try, but how stupid do you think I am to give up on an opportunity to get my revenge?"

"Fine, have it your way." She let go of the staff. It clattered to ground, morphing back into its original form. "Kill me, if that's what you want."

"Gladly." My hand snaked out and grasped her neck.

Aislin's pulse raced under my thumb. I lifted her off the ground. Her legs kicked and hands clawed, but I held tight. Blue energy hissed and crackled, enveloping my whole body. I leaned in and parted my lips.

This was it, the moment I had waited for. I breathed in her scent: fear, pain, pity, and sadness. My lips touched hers. I devoured her essence. She moaned in my arms. Pain shot through my temple.

I cried out, letting her go. Aislin crumbled to the asphalt, face flushed. I stumbled backwards. Pain pierced my skull. What the hell? My throat itched. I pushed out an ear-splitting scream. My vision darkened and blurred. No, this wasn't happening.

"Kaydynce!" Aislin called out, but the premonition took hold.

Blood splattered against the wall. Screams of pain ripped through the air. Bodies piled up around me.

"Run, my queen."

"I won't leave you, Illium!" I clawed my way toward him. Hands pulled me back. I struggled.

Swords clashed and clanked against metal and wood.

War cries echoed through the room.

"Let me go!" More hands grappled onto me.
"Forgive me, my queen." Illium fell to his knees.

Blood spewed from his pale lips. A white blade protruded through his back. The light dimmed from his indigo eyes.
"No!" I screamed. The killer turned, blue eyes widening.

"I'm sorry, Kay."

Chapter 13

I ducked, covering my head as glass shattered around us. Kaydynce's scream echoed down the street. The street lamps around us were gone. The pitch-black night rejoiced.

"Kaydynce?" She didn't move. I crept closer and knelt in front of her. Shaky hands covered her face. "Kaydynce, please say something."

Tears trickled between her fingers. "No, no, no," she mumbled over and over.

I rested a hand on her shoulder. "It's going to be okay."

She stiffened, hands falling away from her face. Watery eyes held my gaze. Kaydynce straightened and slapped my hand away.

Her eyes narrowed. "Don't touch me," she spat, scrambling up.

I winced. She bolted. I stood there for a moment, arms dropping to my sides. What the hell just happened? I sighed.

"Am I stupid for thinking she could change?" I asked the night. "Am I too trusting? Time after time she betrays me, yet I can't let go of the girl she used to be."

Silence greeted me. My shoulders slumped. Yeah, that's what I figured. I fell to my knees and hung my head.

"I miss you, Kaelin." What was I doing? Talking to the dead, apparently.

"I miss you too, Linny."

My head snapped up. I glanced around, heart in my throat. Nothing moved. I closed my eyes. A single tear escaped. I wiped it away, sniffling. It wasn't real, his voice. I clutched my chest. Wood smoke and old leather drifted in the air. My lips trembled. *Damn it, Kaelin, you weren't supposed to die.*

"Don't cry, Aislin. I want to see you smile. You were always breathtaking when you smiled."

I choked out a sob. "You're not real—you can't be. Kaelin is dead."

Thunder rumbled as he laughed. *"Anything is possible, Linny, you should know that by now."*

A hand brushed against my cheek. I reared back. My heart skipped a beat. I searched the night for the source. Could it really be him? I shook my head. Not possible— unless . . . no, why would he have unfinished business?

"If it's really you, then why can't I see you? And why would you show up now? None of it makes sense." My mind flinted through reasons why, but none seemed plausible.

He sighed. Warmth tickled the back of my neck. *"Not important right now. I just need you to do one thing for me."* I nodded. More tears trickled down my cheeks. "Anything."

"Don't give up. We'll see each other soon, I promise."

I let out a shaky breath. "Don't make promises you can't keep," I mumbled.

He chuckled. *"I'd never break a promise to you, Aislin."*

His words swirled around me. A gust of wind slammed into me. I stumbled backwards. The warmth from before vanished.

"Kaelin?" I waited for a reply, but none came. He was gone once more, and I was left alone to my thoughts.

I waited for my pulse to return to normal before embarking back to Remy's studio. It was becoming harder and harder to tell reality from fantasy. Maybe this was a dream. Kaydynce didn't just try to kill me and have her first Death Call, and Kaelin's ghost or whatever never contacted me. It was all a figment of my imagination brought on by guilt and lack of sleep. I sucked in a deep breath and let it out slowly.

I had to tell Remy. There was no escaping that possibility. He would understand—I hoped.

~ ~ ~

"Why didn't you tell me this sooner?" Remy scrambled around his desk. Papers scattered and fluttered to the floor.

"Can you please tell me what's going on?"

He slammed his spell book onto the desk and flipped through the pages, mumbling under his breath.

"If what you say is true, then there might be a way to bring him back to the human realm, for a short period. But that should give us enough time to calculate where he is."

"Woah, hold on—if that's possible then why can't we bring him back completely?"

Remy rubbed his temples. "Time is different in each realm. A few minutes here could be a day there. I have no way of telling. My hope is he's in the in-between realm."

"In-between realm?"

Remy nodded, flipping a couple more pages. He turned the book to face me and pointed. I leaned in, scanning the text.

"You know I can't read that, right?" I crossed my arms over my chest.

"Oh! Um, well what it says is, 'The Realm of In-Between, the place between the living and the dead.' It's basically where the dead go to decide their fate—be it in

Heaven or Hell."

"And how long does that usually take?"

Remy shook his head. "There's no way of telling, as I said before—time moves different in each realm. Could be a day or five years—for all we know he could already be gone."

My heart plummeted. That would mean I'd lost him forever.

"So, if he's not in the in-between, then what?"

"Then there's nothing we can do. I've already used up all the supplies I gathered to open the gateway to Hell. Heaven is impenetrable."

I sighed. "I wouldn't want to take him from Heaven anyways. So that's it, this was all for nothing?"

Remy sat down and clasped his hands together. "Not necessarily. If he's still communicating with you then he has some sort of access point." He pushed up his glasses. "Where have you heard his voice?"

I bit my lip. "Um, the first time was in the . . ." Remy interrupted.

"Wait a minute, you're telling me this wasn't the first encounter?"

I shook my head. "Third actually."

Remy closed his eyes and rested his forehead on his hands. "You should have told me immediately after it happened."

I hung my head. "I-I didn't think it was important."

He lifted his head, eyes narrowing. "Not important? Everything that happens to you is important, Aislin. I need to know every little detail so I can protect you."

I pursed my lips. "I never asked you to protect me."

"That's right, you didn't. I made the decision myself." Remy leaned back in his seat. "Is there anything else you haven't told me?"

I shuffled my feet, not meeting his glare. "Um, I might have had a run-in with Kaydynce."

Remy flung forward, hands slamming against the desk. "What! When? Where?!"

"Woah," I threw up my hands. "Down, boy. To answer your multitude of questions: about an hour ago—a little before I heard Kaelin's voice, and it happened where Kaelin died and I lived."

Remy settled back down. "I really am sorry, Aislin. I wish I could have saved him."

I kept my eyes on my feet. "Me too, Remy. Me too."

"So, what happened? Did she tell you where she's been?"

I shrugged. "Not really, all she said was Illium took care of her."

Remy nodded. "I see. I'm curious to know why she didn't brag to you, her only friend."

"I doubt we're friends now," I mumbled.
"What was that?"

I jumped. "Oh, um, nothing. Uh, she did however, try to kill me."

"What?!"
I flinched. "She didn't hurt me."

"I should hope not or else you wouldn't be standing here right now."

I put my hands on my hips. "What are you trying to say, Remy? You don't think I can beat her?"

He smirked. "Oh, I know you can't."

I balked, throwing my hands in the air. "Oh, thanks for the boost in confidence, Remy, I really needed that."

He chuckled. "Not to say you won't eventually, but right now—I think not." His tone hardened. "I do, however, know if you're going to beat her, you need to toughen up. You can't see her as a friend anymore—it will get you killed."

Chapter 14

Kaydynce

I ran. I ran as fast and as far as my legs would take me before collapsing. My knees slammed to the ground. Pain reverberated through my bones. I winced, but the pain was nothing compared to the ache in my chest.

Tears escaped. Why? I tilted my head back and stared up at the stars. Why here, why now? No answer. I closed my eyes. Anger bubbled to the surface. It was all her fault.

My hands curled into fists. Everything I held dear, she destroyed. I wouldn't let her this time. Illium was mine. Cold droplets dripped against my cheeks. Rain pitter-pattered against the asphalt, slow at first then picked up speed. I ignored the sting. Warmth fled, I shivered.

"Kaydynce." I stiffened.

There was no reason to turn around. I knew that voice. My heart skipped a beat. Would he be mad? I shook my head. Silly question. My name lingered in the air as if waiting for confirmation. I couldn't ignore him. Taking a deep breath, I glanced behind me. My breath caught as our eyes met.

Water skidded down his already wet hair. Indigo eyes were wide and panicked. He was even more handsome in the Human Realm, all wet. His brow creased as he stalked forward. I gulped. Excuses formed in my head.

*I left to find you, I didn't mean to go through the portal—*I doubted he would believe a single one. I waited for the words I knew were coming. *How could you? I told you to stay.*

Silence.

He fell to one knee. His hand cupped my cheek. I leaned into it, relishing his cold touch. For a moment, all my fears disappeared.

"I . . . I found you." His voice shook.

I rested my hand on top of his. Tears threatened to fall. "I'm sorry. Please don't be mad. I know you said to stay, but I just couldn't. Being cooped up inside was killing me. I know it was wrong, but the portal was open and I just wanted to leave and . . ." his chilled lips crashed against mine.

My heart skidded to a halt before picking up a faster tempo. Need and urgency danced between our lips. My grip tightened on his hand as my other pulled at his shirt. Illium shivered. I had never seen him like this. Needy and insistent—the sense of urgency catapulted my pulse higher.

I shifted closer. His other arm snaked around my waist.

"Let's go home," Illium whispered.

I nodded, afraid if I spoke the spell would be broken. He straightened, pulling me with him. My feet lifted off the ground as he held me against his hip. With a wave of his hand, a door appeared. In one stride, we were through. Darkness shrouded us only for a moment. Unlike when I went through on my own, another door came into view immediately.

My heels barely touched the castle floor, before I was bombarded.

"My queen!" Voices exclaimed, a cacophony of noise.

"We were all so worried when you disappeared."

Fairies, imps, and the like, some I wasn't even sure what they were, swarmed me. Tiny hands flitted and fluttered on my arms, legs, and any other body part they could reach. Heat coursed up my cheeks. What was this feeling? Why had they been worried? It wasn't like I had been gone for that long.

"I-I'm fine, thank you," I stumbled over my words a bit. "My queen is quite tired from her journey. She needn't be bothered thus more. We shall take our leave," Illium stated, venom hidden in his words.

A shiver travelled down my spine. Tension hung in the air. An elephant in the room. Nails dug into my hip. A hush fell over the creatures as Illium carted me away. No words were spoken, not even when we entered our private chamber. I nibbled on my lower lip. How long would it last? I fidgeted in his arm. He recoiled, walking to the other side of the bedroom. I fell back against the bed.

He ran his hands through his hair. It was the first time I noticed how disheveled it was. His long, white hair, which was usually tied up loosely against his back, had been set free. Strands stood up—some clung to his pale face and others stuck up from the crown of his head. Illium's clothes were also tousled—wrinkled and wet. His composure was broken, and our subjects had seen it.

Weakness.

I shivered. Kingdoms had fallen because of it. I wouldn't let my reign be one of them. The foot board dug into my lower back. The pain only strengthened my resolve.

"Illium?" My voice came out meek. I ground my teeth. "Illium," I said a bit louder.

Indigo eyes skidded my way, but didn't stay. He kept pacing. I growled, my hands fisting. This was not him. The Illium I knew barely showed emotion. Nothing phased him, until now. Too much emotion flinted across his pale features. Lips pinched, brows furrowed, the constant tick of his fingers digging into his scalp—all spoke volumes.

I crossed my arms over my chest and waited. Time dragged on. No glances, no words. I closed my eyes and sucked in a breath. Weariness settled in my bones. I slumped against the bedframe. This was getting us nowhere.

The strength I had mustered up had fled, along with my voice. My iced heart shattered. A tear fell, splattering on my dress. I had lost. No matter what, he was gone—be it literal or imaginary.

Silence echoed through the room. My eyes snapped open. The shuffling of his feet had stopped. My breath caught. There he stood, blonde hair cascading around his shoulders and angled face. Eyes as intense as ever. My pulse galloped. Here was my king—turbulent as a storm. He stood straighter, hands now tucked behind his back. The only emotion was in his now sapphire blue eyes. I gulped.

"Kaydynce," my name rolled off his tongue, soft with a hint of desperation, "don't ever do such a thing again."

I nodded, unsure of how to reply. The pain in his voice shot through me. I had assumed the ache was my heart being torn into a million pieces, but it was much worse. The ice was melting, little by little.

It had thawed to a point where a new ache grew— infecting it. More tears trickled down my cheeks. I shook my head, blinking them away. A queen didn't cry, yet here I was.

My own hair clung to my wet cheeks. How I must look to him. Blonde hair sticking to any damp surface it could, red, puffy eyes, and my poor, powder blue sundress soaked and covered in dirt. I was a mess. A hot mess, but still messier than I should have been in his presence. A queen was composed and regal—I was neither. I cast my eyes down. Footsteps came closer. His black shoes entered my vision. I didn't look up.

Fingers grazed my jaw. I stiffened and turned away. After such silence, I wasn't about to crumble before him and his cool touch.

"My queen." His voice was as sweet as honey. I scoffed.

"Why so formal, Illium?" I spat his name, finally meeting his gaze. Blue eyes flashed violet.

Chills ran down my spine, but I didn't waver. The corner of his lips lifted slightly. The temperature in the room dropped a couple degrees. I held my ground.

"I see," Illium's fingers coasted down my jawline. My lashes fluttered as heat took the place of the chill. "Defiance is a color few can wear."

I licked my lips. "I can wear any color."

He chuckled, leaning in. "Oh, I am aware." His breath tickled my ear. I shivered.

Anger dissipated. Warmth spread up my body. His desire was palpable, and how could I refuse? Illium's soft touches hardened as his hands curled into my hair. Lips captured mine. I drowned. Fingers burrowed and twisted strands.

Illium's other hand encircled my back, lifting my feet off the ground. I gasped against his lips. He deepened the kiss. Our bodies crashed to the bed. My hands skimmed down his soaked, white shirt to the end. I ripped it open. Buttons scattered across the bed and floor.

A growl reverberated through him and into me. I trembled, need slamming into me like a wave. His own hands untangled themselves to travel down my shoulders to my chest before skipping down my thighs. I couldn't hold back a moan. The lightest of touches sent flames dancing across my skin. He broke away, nibbling on my lower lip.

His mouth trailed cool kisses across my shoulders and down further to the plunged neckline of my dress. Teeth nipped at the straps containing my cleavage. They fell effortlessly, exposing half of my body to his greedy eyes. He sucked in a breath, hands stalling.

I tilted my head to the side, hair falling over to one side. I raised a brow. His Adam's apple bobbed. I giggled, running my hands across his hips and to the button of his pants. This was hardly our first time, yet he always had the same reaction. Awestruck.

"If you want it, take it," I whispered, a smile lifting my lips.

"Gladly," a deep voice said.

Illium's head snapped back to glare at the intruder. I angled my body so I too could see who had interrupted us.

"Though I doubt the king would be very happy with me showing him up. Yet if the queen wishes," he flashed a pearly-white grin, "then I must oblige."

Hazel eyes danced as he waited for a response. Interest piqued, I sat up. The rest of my sundress pooled around my legs. Illium's whole body went rigid. I bit my lip, holding back a giggle.

This intruder wasn't the most repulsive thing I had seen—in fact he was quite handsome. Chestnut brown hair rippled around his strong jawline. A simple green shirt covered his muscular torso and jeans covered the rest. Though I could only imagine what was underneath.

Illium sighed, tucking me behind him as he straightened his back. I peeked at this man from between Illium's shoulder blades.

"My queen," he said through clenched teeth, "I would like to introduce Elijah Hawthorne—the renowned tracker of the Lupine Pack."

Elijah's grin widened as he put a hand over his heart and bowed. I nibbled on my bottom lip.

"It's a pleasure to finally make your acquaintance, though I would have preferred under better circumstances than this."

Elijah straightened and flashed another award-winning smile. "Oh, the pleasure is all mine, my queen." His eyes roamed down my exposed body. I shivered. "I couldn't have asked for a better time."

Illium's jaw twitched out of the corner of my eye. I covered my mouth, hiding a smile. How interesting.

"That is quite enough," Illium inhaled deeply before exhaling. "I do believe you have a task to take care of."

"There are many tasks I'd like to take care of," his voice dropped a few octaves, "but I will do as my king wishes— for now."

My breath fogged in front of me, goose bumps rose on my arms. I shivered. "T-Thank you, E-Elijah, you may go now," my teeth chattered with each word.

He bowed, that same grin on his face, and left.
"M-Maybe, w-we should close the door."

Illium turned, shooting daggers with narrowed eyes before conceding. He slid from the bed with the fluidness of a dancer. His back remained rigid. The door slammed shut with barely a touch of his agile fingers. When he swiveled around, I gasped. Dark as night eyes bore into me. His blonde hair was even more disheveled than before. It swirled around his angular face as if a wind lifted it.

He strode toward me and stopped just short of my feet. Cold fingers wrapped around my ankles and pulled. My feet were against his hips now.

Illium smirked, leaning into me. "You are mine, and only mine."

Harsh lips smothered mine in a kiss full of heat and need. At the same time, his body crashed into mine. I fell into ecstasy.

Chapter 15

Weeks went by without another mishap or encounter. "I still don't understand why I have to continue to train, though."

Remy's lips thinned as he held up the wooden shield one more time. "If you recall, there are quite a few supernatural beings running amuck and causing havoc where ever they go. I would say that's a good enough reason to continue— not to mention, Kaydynce is out there trying to kill you."

I sighed, swinging my bow staff to the right. He blocked, pushing forward. I stumbled back, tightening my grip.

"I know, I know. It's my fault for the release of thousands of creatures." I ran forward, striking to the right then left. Remy blocked the right and dodged the left. "But don't you think I've trained enough?"

Remy charged, shield slamming into my staff. "Nope." I planted my feet and pushed back. We broke apart. "Nobody is ever fully skilled—practice makes perfect."

I ground my teeth, circling him. My eyes searched for any weakness or chink in armor. Remy followed my steps.

"Fine, so what now?" I asked, shoulders tensed.

A grin spread across his lips. "Final showdown. Give me all you've got, then we can take a break."

I laughed, rolling my eyes. "Oh, what? Tired after, what, an hour of cuts and bruises?"

He raised his chin, pushing up his glasses. "Of course not. You, on the other hand, look like death."

The corners of my lips lifted. "Haha, very funny." A low rumble echoed off the walls. I raised a brow. "Oh—now I understand," I shook my head, "you want a break because you're hungry."

The lightest shade of pink tinted his ebony skin. He scoffed. "Absurd. I just think you need a break, you have been through a lot in the past month."

I crossed my arms over my chest. My bow staff rested against my hip. "If you truly thought that then we wouldn't be training, now would we?"

He pursed his lips, but didn't respond.

I nodded. "That's what I thought." Sweat trickled down my temple. "I could use a break though." Remy lowered his shield, smirking.

"Yeah, yeah, whatever," I said, smirking back. "How about we go to that one place you like so much—the place with all the knickknacks."

He shook his head. A frown marred his lips. "Um, I'd rather not."

I reared back, one brow raised. "What? Why not? I thought it was your hang-out spot." My eyes narrowed. I leaned forward. "What did you do?"

Remy shuffled his feet, casting his eyes down. His glasses slid to the tip of his nose.

"I-I may have asked her out—"

"What!?"

"—and stood her up."

My jaw dropped. "Woah, hold up, you did what?!"

He rubbed a hand on the back of his neck. "You had just gotten back, and well, it slipped my mind."

I shook my head and pressed my thumb and index fingers on the bridge of my nose.

"I can't believe something like that slipped your mind— of all the things to forget."

Remy grimaced. "She probably hates me."

"Who could blame her? You did apologize, right?" Remy hung his head, shoulders slumping. "Damn it, Remy!" I threw my hands up in air.

The Leaf Blade clattered to the floor. He flinched. I inhaled slowly then let it out.

"It's fine, we can fix this. When was your date supposed to be?"

"Um, three weeks ago."

"Three weeks! No, it's fine—so it's been three weeks since you last talked to her. I can work with this—we'll just tell her what happened, and it will be . . ." A portal opened up to our left "Now what?" I glared at Remy. "This conversation isn't over."

Squaring my shoulders, I faced the unwanted guests. My face soured, recognizing one of the two men. Indigo eyes twinkled as he bowed.

"Illium," I said, crossing my arms over my chest. I ignored the other.

"Aislin, always a pleasure. You remember Elijah."

My eyes flickered to Elijah, catching on green eyes with flecks of brown. I gulped, eyes darting back to Illium. His lips tilted upwards.

"Yes, I remember. Now why are you here?" I asked— not sure I even wanted to know the answer.

His grin spread. "For you, of course."

I tensed. "What kind of game are you playing at, Illium? I'm tired of being the pawn in your chess game."

Illium's lower lip jutted out. "Oh dear, have I offended the little banshee?" My hackles rose. He chuckled. "Don't worry, it benefits both of us."

I ground my teeth. "Anything that benefits you, I sure as hell don't want."

He raised a brow. "Don't be so hasty to turn this down, Aislin Gray. Elijah here is the best tracker of his kind. Now,

I assume I don't have to tell you what that means."

I crossed my arms over my chest. "Yeah, yeah, I know what that means. What I don't understand is what it has to do with me."

"Ah, but don't you? There is a certain someone whom both of us are trying to find, you see, and my dear Elijah has the capability to track said person. Do you see where I'm going with this yet?" I froze, eyes widening. "There it is. Yes, we can find your precious Kaelin. However, to do such a thing, I need your cooperation."

My eyes narrowed. Suspicion crept into my thoughts. How did I know he was telling the truth? And why was he trying to find Kaelin? There was no good reason for Illium's interest in Kaelin. Elves were manipulators—twisting the truth as much as possible. Yet if Kaelin could be found, then how could I say no? The chances of finding him were slim since I knew he wasn't in Hell. I bit my lip.

"Fine, I'll help. What do you need me to do?"

"Aislin," Remy warned. I brushed him off. If this was the only way, then I would do it.

Illium's grin widened. "Splendid." He bowed and tilted his head toward Elijah. "I, however, have other obligations to attend to. Elijah here will inform you of what is needed and what not to find your sweet love."

He raised a hand. A doorway of blue light appeared behind him. "I bid you adieu, Aislin Gray. I'm sure I'll see you soon." He stepped backwards. The light engulfed him then it disappeared in a blink of an eye.

"Yeah, I didn't want a farewell, anyways," Remy mumbled.

I rolled my eyes then turned to Elijah. His arms were crossed over his chest and the corners of his lips were curved upwards. I frowned. I knew nothing about this tracker or his motives. Blind faith wasn't something I wanted to do again. So why was he here? I studied him, from his posture to every little tick or shift of muscles. A curtain of silence fell.

I nibbled on my bottom lip. Copper filled my mouth. Green eyes flashed. In a split second, he was in front of me. I stumbled back. His hand grabbed my chin as his thumb grazed my lip. I shuddered. My pulse quickened. Our eyes locked and I was drowning. Green and brown danced in his eyes, but then there were also blue flecks, like murky water.

I blinked, shaking off the feeling. "Aislin!" Remy charged forward, but the moment was gone.

I slapped his hand away. He grinned and licked his thumb. It had all happened so fast.

Elijah stepped away, holding up his hands. I stared, mouth hanging open. My breath came out in tattered gasps. I crumbled.

"Aislin?" Remy's voice held caution and worry. I didn't—couldn't look at him.

My eyes were glued to the predator in front of me. All my strength vanished. I was just a girl. I wanted to close my eyes, but if I looked away, who knew what would happen. He was quick and agile, like a wolf. Chills ran up and down my spine. If he chose to, I'd be dead, and nothing Remy could do would prevent it.

He was a weapon, ready to pull the trigger at any time. Fear clawed at my throat. A deep growl reverberated off the walls. I flinched, ducking down.

"What did you do to her?" Remy snapped. I whimpered. Elijah chuckled. "I let her know she isn't invincible. Death comes for everyone. She got lucky in Hell, but luck runs out eventually. It's better she learns that now than when it's too late." He held out a hand. My eyes shifted from his hand to his muddy water gaze. "Don't worry though, I'm not here to bring you to death's door."

I hesitated, but only for a moment. My hand fell into his. Fingers wrapped around my wrist and pulled. I stumbled up. An arm snaked behind my back, steadying me. I nodded, gulping. The corner of his lip tilted up. He let go. I controlled my erratic breathing. Without meaning to, my feet backpedaled a few inches.

"T-Then why are you here?" I hated how shaky my voice was. Pushing down the fear that still rattled around, I straightened.

He may have seen my weakness, but I wasn't about to show it again.

Elijah huffed. "Like the king said, I'm here to track down this Kaelin everyone keeps on talking about, and from what I can gather, you were the closest to him."

I puckered my lips. "I don't know if anyone has told you, but Kaelin is dead. So unless you have some way of tracking a dead man then cool, but if not, then you're wasting your time."

His eyes danced, the grin spreading. "A challenge, nothing more. No worries, princess, I'll find your prince charming—unless I can tempt you to fall for a knight."

My nose wrinkled. "Don't call me that."

He bowed, hand over his heart. "Whatever you say, princess."

I ground my teeth. "Go to Hell." My nerves were already fried, I didn't need anything else plucking at them.

Elijah chuckled. "Already been."

Chapter 16

Aislin

"Are you going to follow me everywhere I go?"

"Yes," Elijah said, nothing more.

"Humph. Aren't you supposed to be tracking Kaelin?" It had only been a couple hours since Illium dropped him off, and he was already getting on my nerves.

"Oh, I am."

My hands balled into fists. There was no point in arguing the fact. His short replies irked me. A man of few words, even though I knew he could be a talker. I shook my head. Night had fallen. The crescent moon cast a soft glow on the deserted street. The Leaf Blade was strapped to my side in its original form.

I scanned the surrounding area. Remy had sent me on another hunt. The target—a pesky pixie. Like fairies, they were mischievous yet usually harmless. There was no telling why this pixie chose to be malicious.

"All right, since you have a better sense of smell than me, I might as well put you to use."

"Nope."

I swiveled around. "Excuse me?"

He grinned. "Not my job, princess."

My eyes narrowed, nostrils flaring. "What did I say about calling me that!" I turned away and walked on. "Whatever, I don't need your help anyways."

Okay, if I was a pixie, where would I go? In a city? Not too many places.

"The park."

I glanced back at Elijah. "What about the park?"

He sighed, as if it was obvious. "The pixie."

I slapped a hand to my forehead, facing forward again. Of course, the park was the perfect place for a pixie. The green grass, small pond, and people—tons of people and animals. The perfect victims. Hopefully it was still there.

"Thanks," I said, frowning. My eyes flickered back to him, "but I thought you weren't going to help me."

He flashed white teeth. "Never said I wouldn't."

My brows flew up. "Um, yeah you did. You said, and I quote, *nope*."

"A guy can change his mind, can he not?" Was there a slight tint to his cheeks? I shook away the thought.

"The park then," I stopped and searched, "which is, where?"

He flung his head back and laughed—deep and throaty. I jumped, pulse racing. I pressed a hand to my heart.

"Warn me next time, please. You nearly gave me a heart attack."

"Sorry, princess, but it's absurd to me that you don't know your way around the city." He bowed. "I may be wrong in this assumption, but shouldn't someone who has grown up here be able to know their way around?"

I pursed my lips, and avoided his quizzical gaze.

"Now he talks," I mumbled under my breath. My eyes flickered back to him.

The faint glow of the moon pooled in his hazel eyes. I turned away, afraid of the way my heart skipped every time our eyes met.

"I only speak when I have something to say—not on command."

I nodded, staring ahead. "Fair enough. I don't suppose you know where the park is?"

"Of course I do, princess, let me just lead the way for you."

"Please tell me you're not being sarcastic." I glanced back for a moment, waiting for his response.

He shrugged. "Of course not."

I snapped my jaw shut. Shaking my head, I turned around again. Pluck, pluck, pluck—that's what he was doing. Something skidded under my feet. I stumbled. Arms wrapped under my chest and pulled. I fell into him. Warmth radiated off his body.

"I-I'm fine. You can let go now." He didn't. If anything, his arms tightened.

"I think we found your pixie," he growled.

I looked up at him. "How . . ." he pointed to his nose.

"Gotcha. Anything else you would like to mention?"

He smirked. "Nope."

I closed my eyes. Once he found Kaelin then I wouldn't have to deal with him ever again. *Focus, Aislin.* Bell-like laughter filled the air. My eyes snapped open.

"There." I pointed to the alley steps away. Translucent wings fluttered before disappearing. "Come on!" I struggled against his iron grip.

Elijah chuckled and dropped his arm. I careened forward. My knee slammed into the sidewalk. I sucked in air through my teeth.

"Oops." I whipped my head around and threw daggers with my eyes. He shrugged, a lopsided grin spreading across his lips.

Asshole.

Another tinkle bounced off the walls. I picked myself up and brushed off my jeans. Amethyst eyes peeked out from behind the wall. Orange hair fell in waves behind its back. I froze.

"I thought you were going to catch it, princess," Elijah whispered. Hot breath tickled my nape. I shivered.

"I am," I said, through clenched teeth.

"Oh, I bet you are. Take your time," he gestured toward the pixie's retreating form. "It's not like it's going to run away or anything."

My hands balled into fists. I spun around. Hazel eyes danced inches away from my face. I tensed—unsure of what he would do. All my anger fizzled out at seeing amusement cross his handsome features. He was teasing me. It should have sparked defiance and more anger, yet it caught me off guard. Who was this guy?

"I hate to interrupt your daydreaming, princess, since I can only assume it's about me, but the pixie is back. I think it brought friends, but who am I to say."

"What?" Elijah swiveled me around. "Oh. Well, shit."

He was right. The pixie came back—with reinforcements. There was a total of six pixies now. Iridescent wings flickered in and out of focus.

"Any bright ideas?" I asked, hands searching for the Leaf Blade at my side.

"How hard could trapping six pixies be?" He glanced my way. "You do have something to capture them with, right?" Capture? My heart sunk. That's what I had forgotten.

"Let me guess, you have no way of containing one pixie, much less six."

I bit my lip. "I may have left the jar Remy gave me in his office."

Elijah shook his head. "Great, that's just great, princess. Now what? I doubt you want their blood on your precious hands."

I bristled. "For your information, I've killed my fair share of supernatural beings."

"I'm not going to disagree with you, but as far as we know, they are innocent of any crime other than mischief.

Would you kill them, just for that?"

"No." I couldn't, *wouldn't* do that.

"That's what I thought. Now then, so far, they haven't done anything, except if you count staring evilly with their purple eyes. I suggest we come up with a plan—fast."

"No need to remind me," I mumbled, scrambling to find a solution.

My eyes zipped around the area: alley to the left, vacant street beyond—there! A yard away to our right was a box.

"Keep them distracted for a moment. I have an idea."

"Better be a damn good one, princess." He charged forward "I have no patience for flies."

"Who you calling flies!" One of them squeaked. I didn't wait for a reply.

I veered to the right and ran. Screeches and growls echoed through the air. I cringed, but didn't stop. If he could hold them off, then maybe this could work. As the box entered my line of sight, the noises quieted. Shit. Now that I could see it fully, I knew it wouldn't work. The bottom had been ripped out. There was no way to close it. Think. My eyes fell on a tattered blanket a few feet away.

That would do. I snatched it up, along with the box.

"Hey!" someone called.

"I'll give it back, I promise!" I called back.

God, I hoped they all fit. The box was about the length of my legs to my hip. Pixies weren't all that big in their normal form. Some had the ability to become human-sized, but thankfully not all. I glanced at Elijah and the pixies. I bit back a laugh.

Three of the pixies, in various sizes, were clinging to his hair—ripping and pulling what they could. The other three were latched to his legs—two on his left and the third on his right. Pastel colored hair bobbed and weaved as Elijah swatted at them.

I slowed my pace. Green-yellow eyes flashed, narrowing. A deep growl reverberated through the air. The lamps flickered. A violet haired pixie went flying—slamming into the stone wall by the alley.

"Any time now, princess!" he snapped, canines glistening in the dull light.

Right. I shot forward, circling him. Tiny, sharp teeth sank into his calf. I winced. Elijah howled. He plucked up a pink haired one by the wings and flicked it. The thing tumbled toward me. With the box under my arms and blanket tucked around the bottom, I stumbled forward. With a soft oomph, it landed against the blanket.

One down, five more to go. Elijah struggled with the other four. The pixie that had hit the wall lay unmoving. I'd pick it up later. The night had gone quiet, except for the tinkling laughter and frustrated growls.

There wasn't any way I could help. If I set the box down, the one pixie I had caught might escape. Elijah was handling it well anyways. No need to interrupt. The pixies, however, were getting smarter—flitting in and out of his reach, nipping at his out-stretched hands.

The whole scene was comical. He roared, claws lengthening, and swiped. A blue haired pixie collided with a yellow haired one. Both swirled to the ground. I snatched them up. Two more and we would be done. The moon had risen higher in the sky. The faint, silvery light bounced off the last two sets of wings. I shielded my eyes. Elijah didn't have that luxury.

The pixies darted forward, teeth snapping at any exposed skin. He lifted his arms and covered as much of his face as he could. They were screeching now—ear-splitting screams. Their wings zipped in and out of focus. If it wasn't for their hair, I wouldn't be able to see them at all.

Elijah fell to one knee. I bit my lip. Just two more, that was it. I squared my shoulders and charged, yelling a battle cry. Both pixies stopped mid-bite. Amethyst eyes locked onto me. I gulped, but kept on running. They scattered. I stood in front of Elijah and glared at the remaining two. One of them was the target. Its orange hair swayed with its body.

"All right, I need you two to get in the box. We've taken down the rest of your little group already. There's no point in fighting anymore."

The pixie beside the orange one glanced at her then retreated. Claws dug into its wings. It cried out. Without a second thought, Elijah threw it into the box.

I raised a brow. The target's wings fluttered once before drooping. It glided into the box. I covered it completely. I wiped a hand across my brow.

"Awesome, now that that is over, I need a nap."

"I think I need some kind of disinfectant. Those nasty little beasts have quite a bite."

I laughed, shaking my head. "I think Remy has some peroxide in his first-aid kit. Now let's get the hell out of here."

"Don't forget," he pointed at the violet haired one, "that one."

I nodded. "Yeah, probably best if I didn't. I'd hate for more of them to come after us because I'd forgotten one."

"That would be your fault, not mine."

Chapter 17

Aislin

"That's the last of them—pesky pixies. You sure they don't have any sort of disease?" Elijah rubbed his calf.

The bite was inflamed, that was for sure. It was red and puffy, like most of the scattered nips. It took three hours to lug the pixies back to home base. They buzzed like angry bees—kicking and screaming against the blanket. Remy had greeted us the minute we walked in. We stood in the middle of the training room as Remy examined our catch.

"None that the books say. Though, I wouldn't be surprised if their saliva held a multitude of bacteria. Nothing to worry about. Apply this salve every so often," Remy tossed a small vial into the air. Elijah caught it without missing a beat. "And you should be fine."

Elijah nodded, unscrewing the cap. He wrinkled his nose.

"It's floral—too floral," Elijah's nostrils twitched before he sneezed. "So many scents."

"It's only a bit of calendula flower, olive oil, plantain, a table spoon of tamanu oil, some beeswax pastilles—oh and lavender oil, along with a pinch of rosemary antioxidants."

"Oh, is that all?" He rubbed a hand down his face.

"Yes, matter of fact it is," Remy huffed, crossing his arms over his chest.

I sighed. "Can we please get back to the matter at hand?" I gestured to the box a foot away. "What are we supposed to do with six agitated pixies?"

Remy waved a hand. "Oh, that's simple. I'll just teleport them back to the Other Realm."

I blinked. "I don't know if I heard you correctly. Did you just say teleport them?" He nodded. I ran my tongue across my teeth. "Let me get this straight, you can teleport things now? Then why the hell have I been walking everywhere, when you could have just teleported me back?"

"We've talked about this already, Aislin. It's not really teleporting per say, it's more of a relocation spell. Besides, relocating a person is trickier—what with the possibility of something being misplaced or—"

"But you can *relocate* pixies, which are tiny people, with no problem?"

Remy pushed up his glasses, which had slid down slightly. "That is precisely what I'm saying. The smaller the object, the easier it moves."

I brushed a lock of hair out of my eyes. "Fine, you win this time."

He chuckled. "I always win."

"Anything else?" Elijah asked.

We both turned toward him. He smeared some of the salve onto his arm and grimaced. I rolled my eyes. Wimp.

"Do you need help?" He glanced up—hazel eyes meeting mine. A grin spread across his lips.

"Who's asking?" He straightened. "Cause if it's you then yes."

I shifted, putting my weight and arm onto my right hip.

"If it's something perverted then no I'm not helping, but if you can't reach an area then maybe I can offer my services." He didn't respond.

"I'm just going to take these," Remy picked up the box of pixies, "to my office, so I can relocate them."

The blanket shifted as the box moved about. I ignored him and focused more on Elijah. Footsteps receded. I sighed. He would probably be in his office the rest of the night. Silence settled around us. Some unspoken feelings hung in the air. I shook my head. Strands of my hair slapped against my face.

"You know what, never mind." I tucked my hair behind my ear "Forget I even asked."

I stalked off. Mr. Talkative wasn't very talkative anymore. Why did I even bother? I try to do something nice and get crap for it.

"W-Wait." I paused, half-turning. "Do you think you could, um, get my back?"

The corners of my lips curved upwards. He was a beaten dog. His shoulders hunched, and his head lowered. All cockiness had fled. In its place was someone who needed help. This was real—the realest part I had seen. I relished in it. This man who had the ego and charm to sweep any girl off their feet, and he was conceding—to me.

I shrugged. "Yeah, sure, why not."

Elijah's head snapped up, eyes wide. Brown hair fell across his face. His jaw dropped. I crossed my arms and raised a brow.

"Is something wrong?"

He blinked. "Oh, uh, wow. I didn't think you would actually agree."

I blew air out my nose. "Um, I am a nice person, you know." I raised a hand and twirled it. "Now, spin around so

I can get your back."

He tensed. "Um, actually, never mind I . . ."

"You asked for my help." I pointed a finger at him, glaring. "So I'm going to help you."

Elijah wrinkled his nose. "All right, miss bossy, but can we sit for this?" His lips curved up slightly. Hazel eyes dragged down my body. I shivered, tightening my arms around myself.

"I'd hate for me to turn on you, if you happened to hit a sensitive spot. Sitting, however, lowers the risk, but," his eyes danced, "only by a little bit."

I scoffed. "I could take you in a heartbeat."

His right brow lifted. "Oh, is that so? If I remember correctly," he took a step closer, "your fight and flight instincts kicked in not too long ago, and you chose flight— though it was more like frozen to the spot with fear."

I gulped. He was calling my bluff. I straightened, squaring my shoulders.

"Try me."

Elijah threw back his head and laughed. It rumbled like thunder a mile away. Chills ran up and down my arms. My chest clenched. Thoughts of Kaelin flooded my mind. I stumbled backwards.

"Aislin?" it was the first time he had used my name. My throat tightened. Tears threatened to fall. I couldn't answer him.

Flashes of Kaelin and I as kids, the day he got his rusty ass truck, our first kiss—every memory of us together. I spiraled and crashed. My knees slammed into the ground. I covered my ears, wishing the images away.

This wasn't happening, not now. I shook my head, digging my nails into my scalp. It was a movie of our life together. A strangled cry left my lips. Kaelin's death—the last reel of the tape.

"Princess, can you hear me?" I hauled up my gaze. Tears trickled down my cheeks, and he was right there.

Green eyes with flecks of brown and blue searched my face. He rested a hand on my cheek. All my strength disappeared—no fight left. I had failed him. Kaelin's death played on repeat. The one Death Call I couldn't prevent, after the countless others I had. Golden eyes dimming, and his mouthed words *I'm sorry*. The world spun.

"Aislin!"

A voice called to me. I searched through the emptiness. Always searching. Who was I looking for? I couldn't remember. The void dragged on with no purpose. Did I have a purpose? No, I had nothing. There was no time or space— just emptiness. Nothing grew or took shape. I floated on. Pain laced through my head. My breath caught—unable to release.

"Aislin!"

My eyelids flew open. A deep, low growl shook my bones. Black eyes watched me. My heart raced. I tried to scramble up, but couldn't. My body wouldn't work. I was frozen to the spot. The thing sat on my chest, cocking its head to the side. It smiled—rows of tiny, razor sharp teeth gleamed. Pointy ears twitched, but its stare stayed on me. I sucked in a breath. My chest burned. I breathed out, but no air was released. I wheezed.

The growl intensified. The hairs on my arms rose. Out of my peripheral, a snout appeared—teeth bared. I shifted my gaze back to the thing on top of me. It was a greyish color. If it wasn't on my chest I would have never seen it. A shadow with teeth and pointed ears. Its eyes were now fixed on the beast beside me. I followed suit.

Chestnut brown fur stuck up higher on the wolf's nape. Hazel eyes glistened. Saliva dripped from his fangs. My instincts screamed for me to run. I struggled to move and breathe. Black spots entered my vision.

The wolf snapped its jaw closed. The creature stayed put. The beast's ears flattened against its scalp. It lunged. The shadow screeched and swiped at the wolf with claws. Pressure lifted off my chest, but only for a moment. I didn't care. I gobbled up as much oxygen as I could.

The wolf reared back then lunged again. Canines sunk into the creature. It screamed. Crunch.

The room fell silent. The shadow slumped in the wolf's mouth. It disintegrated like ashes in the wind. The remains fluttered to the ground then vanished as if it hadn't been there at all. I shivered and sat up. Yellow green eyes landed on me. It licked its jowls.

I scrambled away, my back hitting the wall. My pulse raced. The hackles on his neck settled down. He sat on his haunches, cocking his head to the side. His tongue lolled out. The most unthreatening posture possible for a wolf, other than on its back. It took a moment for my heart to calm enough for me to figure out what the hell had happened.

"E-Elijah?" I asked.

He barked. I shook my head. "Can you change back, please?"

The wolf whined, lowering himself to the floor. The fur on his body receded, in its place tan flesh. Chestnut brown hair hid his face as wolf ears disappeared once more. Bones snapped and popped. I gaped. He was completely naked. I covered my eyes.

"Um, can you put clothes on?"

A wheezy chuckle filled the room. Something shifted and shuffled. I peeked through my fingers at his retreating form. Pale scars marred his back. I could only assume it was from constant fighting. He bent and picked up something from the ground. I covered my eyes again as he turned. Heat coursed up my cheeks.

"You can look now," Elijah said, chuckling a bit more.

I lowered my hands and gulped. He stood in front of me, shirtless. I hadn't heard his approach at all. Of their own accord, my eyes travelled across his physically fit arms and chest. I bit the inside of my lip. He brushed hair out of his eyes. The movement caught my attention. My eyes snapped up to his. I fell into murky water—green with flecks of blue and brown.

He crossed his arms over his chest and raised a brow. I turned my head away.

"Um, thanks," I said, tucking a strand of hair behind my ear, "for, you know, putting on clothes, and saving me."

Elijah bowed, arm extended. "My pleasure, princess."

I wrinkled my nose. "Stop calling me that." The pet name grated on my nerves.

The corners of his lips curved upwards. He straightened, arms falling back to his sides.

"Nope."

Grrr. "Whatever. Anyways, what the hell was that thing?"

Elijah ran a hand through his hair. "My guess is a mare.

The epitome of the word nightmare."

My mouth fell open. "Um, what?"

He sighed. "A mare—Germanic/Scandinavian demon, which causes nightmares by sitting on the victim's chest and pretty much suffocating them."

My hand went to my throat. A demon almost killed me—in my sleep. I shivered.

"Oh."

Elijah nodded. "Yeah, nasty creatures," he shook his head and grinned. "Thankfully, my sense of smell is on point," his lips curved down slightly. "I did, however, catch a whiff of something else. I can't be sure, but before you passed out earlier, I thought I smelled leather."

I froze. Worn leather. I closed my eyes and pictured him. Kaelin. A sly grin, dancing golden eyes, red-brown hair falling just below his ears, and the aroma of worn leather and wood smoke that clung to every part of him. The longer I imagined him, the more I thought I could hear his deep, thunder-like laughter and booming voice.

"Aislin," Elijah warned. My eyes snapped open. He had only used my name once before.

My gaze landed on him. Elijah's shoulders tensed and his hands flexed in and out of a fist. I followed his eyes. My breath caught.

"Hi, Linny."

Chapter 18

Aislin

This was a dream—I was still dreaming. There was no way. He couldn't be—not here. The world spun around me.

I swallowed.

"K-Kaelin?"

I stepped forward. Elijah held out an arm. I glanced up at him. His brow was furrowed and lips drawn tight.

"Who is he?" Kaelin asked, golden eyes narrowed.

My heart pounded against my chest. Was that jealousy? I wanted to laugh at the absurdity of it.

"None of your business," Elijah growled, stepping in front of me.

I pursed my lips, stepping back around him. "What are you doing? This is who you've been tracking."

Green eyes glared down at me as he dragged me back behind him. I struggled.

"Get your hands off her!"

Elijah let go. I pulled my arm back and punched him. "What the hell?!"

He pressed his fingers against the bridge of his nose. "That's not Kaelin."

Kaelin's lips pulled back and snarled, "Damn dog." He wrinkled his nose. "Disgusting beasts. I don't know how anyone can stand to be around them."

Elijah bent his knees. "I could say the same to you, fox," he spat.

"Wait, what?" My head spun. Fox? What was that supposed to mean?

Kaelin laughed, but it wasn't his. It was light and feathery.

"She's not very bright, now is she?" He shook his head. Black hair cascaded down his back, replacing his normal red-brown hair.

My mouth fell open. The rest of him morphed. Ivory skin, bright red lips, and black ears popped up on top of his head. Kaelin had transformed into a completely different person and gender. Before me stood a tiny woman with the same golden eyes.

"Kitana, always a pleasure to see you."

She chuckled, brushing a hand through her hair. "Indeed. When was the last time? I can't seem to recall."

My eyes flickered from this woman to Elijah. How did he know her? He rolled his shoulders, but kept his stance.

"Your hardened gold eyes watched as Tamal ripped out my throat, if I remember correctly. Fucking snitch."

Her eyes narrowed, ears flattening to her skull. "Tamal fed me, and treated me like family—unlike the rest of the pack."

"Yeah, if family slept with each other."

She continued. "How could I allow a lowly delta mate with the alpha female? It was against pack code—everyone knew that!"

"Ha, you were just jealous I chose Ballia over you. Poor little Kitana, abandoned by her mother and left to die— no one cares."

Kitana lifted her chin and stared him down. "I may have been abandoned, but I didn't die—thanks to Tamal."

"Um, excuse me?" Two sets of eyes turned to me. "Can someone tell me what the hell is going on here?"

Kitana covered her mouth. "Oh my, please forgive me." Her golden eyes brightened as she bowed. "Kitana Cain, at your service."

I crossed my arms over my chest. "No offense, but I don't care who you are. All I care about is why you're here and impersonating Kaelin."

Elijah snorted. Kitana's eyes narrowed. She put a hand on her hip.

"Well if you must know, I'm here for him." She tilted her head toward Elijah. "Word around the street is you escaped Hell. Tamal sent me to see if it was true. Lo and behold, here you are," she scrunched up her nose, glancing around. "Wherever *here* is."

I ground my teeth. "That doesn't explain why you were pretending to be Kaelin."

Kitana cocked her head to the side. Black ringlets fell over her shoulder. She batted her eyelashes.

"I have no idea what you're talking about, dearie, or who this Kaelin is."

My hands balled into fists. I took a step forward. She yawned, patting her mouth.

"Boring!" She sauntered forward, examining her nails. "I was hoping for a bit more excitement."

"I'll show you excitement," I mumbled, glaring at her perfect figure.

Kitana giggled. "Spunky. Now I see why you two are together."

I gaped, eyes widening. "What!?"

Elijah ran a hand down his face. "It's not like that."

She raised a brow. "Isn't it though? I assume that's why you're here, shirtless I might add, and reeking of her."

Heat coursed up my cheeks. I closed my mouth. What could I say to that?

He huffed. "You act like I hit on every girl I meet."

I turned to him and glared. Tinkling laughter filled the room.

"Well, of course you do. You are a predator, after all. Mating is essential for survival, which means you have to actually get a girl to procreate."

"I think I'm going to be sick," I grumbled, holding my stomach.

"Enough!" Elijah snarled.

Kitana's ears flattened against her scalp. "Party pooper."

"You should be glad I haven't snapped your neck yet, Kitana." She held her head up higher, still messing with her nails.

"As if you could."

Elijah shook his head. "That's beside the point. You found me. Hurray. Now go be a good little fox and run back to your master."

The air crackled. The hairs on my arms rose. Kitana's golden eyes darkened, face contorting.

"Tamal is not my master!" she spat. "No one controls me." I rolled my eyes. Overdramatic much? Elijah laughed. Chills ran down my spine. There was no humor in his laugh. It was cold and harsh, unlike the guy I had become accustom to.

"We all have a master—the one who pulls the strings in our sad existence."

Kitana flipped her hair off her shoulder. "When did you become so cynical?"

"When my alpha murdered me." No emotion, no cockiness—nothing. Who was this man?

She rolled her eyes. "Whatever." Kitana moved closer until she was inches away from him.

He tensed. I reached for the Leaf Blade at my side. My fingers grasped air. I gulped. Where had I put it?

"I'll leave," she said, running a polished nail down his bare chest. "But when you tire of the banshee, you know where to find me."

Elijah grabbed her wrist. "Don't worry, I won't." He threw her hand away.

I glanced between the two of them. Tension rippled through the air for a moment before it disappeared.

"Goodbye, Kitana."

She sighed, but her lips curved upwards. "It was good to see you again, Elijah."

Her eyes flickered my way before she sashayed pass, body shrinking.

"Wait!" I called. She paused, glancing over her shoulder. "You never answered my question—why were you impersonating Kaelin?"

She giggled, her black hair turning to fur. Everything about her changed. The tiny woman was gone and in its place sat a fox with three tails. I blinked. Elijah huffed behind me. The fox tilted its head and yipped. I frowned.

"Don't waste your breath. She can't talk in this form." The fox growled then yipped again. Elijah let out a breath. "Fine, I'll tell her." He turned to me. "She may not be able to speak English, but I can understand her language."

"Um, okay."

Kitana yipped and growled then howled. Elijah ran a hand down his face. "I don't think that's going to make her feel any better," he said, "but anyways, she says she's an illusionist—like most kitsunes—I think *trickster* is more accurate, but that's beside the point. The reason she looked and talked like Kaelin was because that's what you wanted to see."

My brows furrowed. "I . . . so none of it was real?"

He shook his head. My heart plummeted. Kaelin hadn't been here—the sweet scent of wood smoke, the rumble of his laughter. I closed my eyes. He was never coming back. My legs gave out. Strong arms caught me, but it didn't matter—

nothing did. None of it was true—all the times I heard him was fake—an illusion, only I could hear and see.

Chapter 19

Elijah

Aislin collapsed. My arms instantly wrapped around her shoulders and under her legs, lifting her to my chest. Heat rolled off Aislin's still form. I gulped. Honeysuckle wafted through the air. I breathed it in. Aislin's scent.

Damn it Kitana, did you have to shatter the poor girl's world? Now what the hell was I supposed to do? I closed my eyes. Every sense was on high alert. Every sound, every touch. My arm tingled where her mahogany hair grazed my bare skin. This was not part of the plan. Find Kaelin— that was it. Babysitting? Not part of the deal. Warm hands touched my chest. I tensed, eyes snapping open.

I searched Aislin's face, noticing for the first time the silky cream skin. Her eyes were still closed, but she had shifted closer. My pulse spiked. When was the last time I was ever this close to someone? Before my untimely death of course, but had it ever felt like this? Warm, soft skin pressed against mine. The quiet whisper of a heartbeat. I sighed. Mixing work with pleasure was off the table, but . . .

I shook my head. Nope, not going to happen. I strode over to the makeshift bed and set her down. A whimper escaped her pink lips. Long lashes fluttered, but remained closed. I let out a breath. A strand of hair slipped down her cheek. Without a second thought, I brushed it back behind her ear. Her skin was like satin beneath my fingertips.

I stepped away. Too close. My heart thrashed in my ears. Honeysuckle engulfed me. I groaned and ran a hand through my hair. This was not supposed to happen. I turned to go.

"Elijah?" The barest of whispers. I glanced back. Misty blue eyes searched mine. "Is any of this real?"

My heart clenched. "Go back to sleep, princess."

She nodded and rested her head on the pillow again. I left. There was no reason to stay. No Kaelin, no job. I ran a hand through my hair as I pushed through the exit. Everything was a mess. I stopped and glanced back at the building I had spent most of my second life at. Nothing special about it.

Grey building attached to another grey building. I shook my head.

"Leaving so soon?" I tensed.
"Illium." Fuck.

Illium leaned against the side of the building, arms crossed over his chest.

A grin spread across his angled face. Indigo eyes narrowed. "I hope you're not leaving for good."

I gulped and straightened. "About to go tracking, actually."

It wasn't a lie, but it also wasn't the full truth.

He nodded. "Good. I wouldn't want to displease my queen and neither should you. She has a nasty temper," his grin widened, "and hunger."

I held back a shudder. "I understand."

"Good. Has there been any progress?"

That was the big question, wasn't it? Progress. "No. Still no sign of him. Had a possible sighting, but it was a bust."

Illium nodded once. "I see. Well, my queen is waiting.

Call if you find him."

I licked my lips. Throat drying. "Will do."

Illium lifted his hand and a doorway appeared. Without a second glance, he walked through. The door vanished with him. My shoulders sagged. Well, fuck.

~ ~ ~

Two days went by since Illium's visit, still no sign of Kaelin. Maybe there was no point, but I had to do something. Not just to save my skin, but for Aislin too. Ever since her reality snapped, she was a shell of her former self. Every vacant glance, hollow laughter—it killed me to see her this way.

I avoided her most of the time, not like it was hard to do. Aislin's fragile body stayed mostly in bed. Her mind was locked up inside. Remy and I kept busy. He did whatever wizards did, and I tracked. Well, tried to track. Ghosts didn't have a scent, or at least as far as I knew. The scene of the crime was my best bet, but even that was a bust. Whatever scents were left from his death had been washed away a year ago.

My hands balled into fists. This was useless! Sighing, I checked on Aislin. She was exactly where I'd left her—curled up on her makeshift bed. I knelt in front of her and studied her pale features. Cloudy blue eyes stared back at me.

"Hey, princess."
She blinked, but didn't reply.
"Have you eaten today?" I asked.
Silence filled the room. I ran a hand down my face.

"Aislin, you have to give me something . . . please." Her sadness seeped into her scent—wilting honeysuckles.

"No," she said, voice barely above a whisper.

I let out a breath. "Okay, let me find you something really quick."
I turned. A hand wrapped around my wrist. My eyes snapped to hers.

"Don't go," she mumbled, tears pricking on her lashes.

A lump formed in my throat. I nodded. The corner of her lips lifted slightly. My heart jumped. She tugged on my arm.
"Stay with me . . . just for a moment . . . until I fall asleep."
I couldn't say no—didn't want to say no. Nodding, I curled up behind her, my arm around her waist. She sighed.
Every day after that I'd go tracking then lay with her until she fell asleep. I knew then what my second chance was.

Chapter 20

Aislin

Days went by, some longer than others. The days soon turned to weeks, then months without any clues or signs of Kaelin, not even the voices. Maybe Kitana had been right— it had all been an illusion made in my own mind.

I sighed and stared up at the popcorn ceiling. What was considered real anyways? Anything? For all I knew, I could still be in the Abyss, the void of space and time—floating in my head. Anything was possible. Craziness was what a person perceived it to be. If that was true, then that meant Kaelin was still alive—somewhere. Had he forgotten me yet? I stretched out my hand above me and examined my fingers. Pink flesh.

Was I even real? Laughter bubbled up.
"All right, get up."

I turned my head to the left even though I knew who it was. Remy glared down at me with his hands on his hips. I groaned and lowered my hand over my face.

"Why?" It wasn't like I had something important to do or anything.

"You know why, Aislin."

I breathed in and let it out. "Yeah, yeah, life goes on— blah, blah, blah."

"Elijah, can you help me out here?" He was still here?

I peeked through my fingers. Hazel eyes held my gaze. I gulped. Flashes of blurry images flickered in my mind: Elijah holding me, his warmth soothing as I drifted to sleep.

I looked away. Why couldn't he have left? It wasn't like he had a reason to be here anymore. If he was even here to begin with. I nibbled on my lower lip.

"You've been grieving long enough, princess. Time to get back to work."

I shook my head and turned away. "No."

A collective sigh escaped their lips. "All right then, you leave me no choice." Hot hands slid under my legs and back. "Up we go."

I squirmed, but soon gave up. My hands rested in my lap. Waves of heat rolled off his skin as he pulled me close. I rested my head against his chest. There was strength and comfort in his arms. I drank it in.

"Has she eaten today?" Elijah asked. I closed my eyes. Had I? "That's what I thought. Right then, let's get some food in your belly. But first, you might need a shower."

Shower. I wanted to laugh. Did I smell that bad? Maybe to him—Mr. Sensitive Nose. I opened my eyes and was captured once again by murky water. Heat burned up my cheeks. Stubble grazed his chin and jawline. I raised my hand, fingers skipping across his skin. He inhaled, closing his eyes. I took the opportunity to study him further.

Chestnut brown hair stuck up all over his head. It stopped just inches above his ears. He was shirtless, yet again.

"I'm just going to set you down now." He licked his lips. A whimper escaped my lips. Elijah bent and placed my feet on the ground.

His arm stayed around my back. I stumbled. His grip tightened on my side.

"I'm fine," I mumbled. Black dots swirled in my vision. No point in telling him that though.

"Do you think you can manage to walk to the showers?"

"I'm not a child!" I snapped, regretting it immediately.

Elijah's eyes narrowed. "Now you've done it," Remy said.

"Oh, forgive me, princess, but you are one. An adult wouldn't pout and throw a tantrum just because she found out something she didn't like. Grow the hell up. This world isn't fit for weaklings—so suck it up, buttercup, or you won't last. I'm surprised you've lasted this long," he extended his arm out, encompassing the whole room. "Life is hard. People die, people suffer—nothing you can really do about that except live. Live like it's your last. Not everyone gets that opportunity."

I pursed my lips. He was right, but . . . I shook my head. "How?"

The corners of his lips curved up. "Forget the good, forget the bad—stop thinking and start doing. I sure as hell am." He winked. "I got a second chance and I'm not going to waste it."

"But what . . ."

"No buts." He grinned. "Don't worry, I'll still look for Kaelin. You, on the other hand," he pushed me forward, "need to get out there and just live."

I stumbled forward, barely catching myself. I turned and glared at him. He shrugged.

"That's all well and good, but first take a shower and get dressed. We have other matters to deal with," Remy said, shooing me away.

I bowed my head and shuffled off.

"Do you think she'll be okay?" I heard Remy ask. I didn't hear Elijah's response, but I could only guess.

My feet took the lead. There was no thinking, just doing. The shower room came into view. Stalls lined the right side where the toilets were and further back were the showers. I stepped into one of the squares that separated each shower, but held no other privacy. It was just a few shower heads attached to the wall—nothing more.

I turned the knob and waited. Water sputtered out. I stepped back and stripped. My clothes clung to my skin. Might need to wash those. I reached into the water. Hot droplets spattered my hand. Steam swirled. I charged in. The hairs on my arms rose as the warm water hit my cool skin. I tilted my head back. The heat eased my aching muscles. I closed my eyes and savored it. The sting of the water, the soft touch of droplets trailing down my arms, and the pain, which slowly subsided.

I ran my hands through my tangled hair, freeing the knots that had formed from my restless sleep. When was the last time I'd showered? I shook my head. Water slung off my hair. I couldn't remember. It didn't matter.

I massaged my fingers through my hair and turned around. Warmth spread across my chest and stomach. Water trickled down. I wrapped my arms around myself. The water cascaded around me, splashing over my face and head.

I sucked in a breath and let it out. Live life—that's what Elijah said. Could I do it, though? I spent a year and some change trying to find Kaelin, was it finally time to let go? My chest tightened. Move on—was that what I needed to do?

Tears pooled in the corner of my eyes, but didn't fall. I wasn't sure if I had the strength to give in.

"Don't give up on us, Aislin."

My eyes snapped open, heart pounding. No. It wasn't real. I laced my fingers in my hair and held my head. Not real. I bowed my head. He isn't here, that's not his voice. I rocked myself under the water.

"You're not real. This is an illusion—a sick and twisted one."

Laughter rumbled. I shivered despite the heat.

"This isn't an illusion, Linny. I may not be here physically, but I'm still with you."

"No. Stop this. Please, I'm so tired." The tears escaped. Pain ripped through my chest. "Not real. You're not real." I shook my head over and over. "This isn't real. You're dead! You're not here!" I screamed.

My throat tightened. Tears streamed down my cheeks. My fingers burrowed themselves further into my hair. Footsteps pounded against the floor. I crouched down and wrapped my arms around my legs. I tucked my head between my knees.

"Linny, please."

"Not real." I giggled. "Nothing is real." My head swam.

Black spots flickered in and out of my vision. I blinked them away, but it wasn't long before they were back. My chest burned. I sucked in a breath. The pressure disappeared, along with the spots. I breathed in and out. My heart thrashed against my sternum.

"Linny."

I rocked back and forth on the balls of my feet. This wasn't happening. None of it was real. The words repeated over and over in my head. The voice of Kaelin persisted.

"Damn it, Aislin, I am real—just not physically. I'm not a figment of your imagination or whatever." He sighed.

"Just don't stop searching, okay?"

"Searching. Searching—always searching," I mumbled.

What was I looking for? The nightmare played out in my head. Lost in nothingness, trying to find something or someone. I didn't know what or who. Ice washed over me. I shivered. The warm water was gone. The footsteps stopped.

"Aislin!" Elijah's alarmed voice captured my attention.

I raised my gaze. It took me a moment to register him. He stood in the doorway, claws gripping the frame. Ragged breaths escaped his lips. Water caught in my lashes. I blinked them away. Goosebumps rose on my arms. The steam drifted then dispersed. Numbness washed over me. More tears threatened to fall. I tightened my grip on my legs.

He let go of the doorframe and walked in. His body tense and ready for a fight. The corner of my lips lifted just an inch.

"Sorry."

Elijah shook his head. He scanned the room, hazel eyes alert. When nothing out of the ordinary popped out, his eyes landed back on me. Murky water turned forest green. My breath hitched.

"I, um," he gulped, Adam's apple bobbing. "Are you okay?"

I nodded, water splashing. The cold barely registered anymore as I stared into his darkening eyes. Eyes I could fall into.

"Yeah," I ducked my head, cheeks burning. "Just thought I heard someone is all."

"R-right, uh, then I guess I'll let you get back to, um, your shower."

I didn't reply. His footsteps receded. I let out a breath, shoulders sagging. With stiff muscles, I stood. The freezing water cooled down the warmth that rose from my skin. That was close. Not only had I been staring at him, heart pounding in my ears, but I was naked. If I hadn't been crouched and covered, he would have seen it all. I grimaced. That thought alone left me weak-kneed.

Naked—in front of Elijah. A werewolf. A predator. I could only imagine what would have happened if he stayed. Heated words. Lingering stares. Then the inevitable kiss—I shook the thought away. That would never happen—not in a million years. Yet . . . those arms, and those eyes—ugh.

I turned the water off. It sputtered before it stopped.

What the hell was I doing? I already knew the answer. Moping around, hoping for a clue or sign, but why? I ran a hand down my left arm, hugging it against my ribs. Why couldn't I move on? A year and a half was long enough to wait. Pressure built in my temples. Ugh, a splitting headache.

Sighing, I wrung out my hair. Droplets plopped on the tile. What was I supposed to do now? Give up on the love of my life or hold out just a little bit longer? Yet, if none of this was real then why try? Moving on seemed like the better option. My heart clenched. Was I really going to do it?

So many questions with no answer. Don't think, just do. Wise words from a wolf with a second chance. I stepped out of the shower and glanced around. Damn it. I hung my head. No towels or clothes. Unless sweaty, who knew how long I'd been wearing them clothes counted.

There was no way I could walk out there wearing nothing but my birthday suit. I bit my lip. No choice. My eyes landed on the heap of dirty clothes inches away. With a grimace, I put them on. Thankfully the clothes were dark. Black tank top and dark blue jeans—the underwear was a different matter. I shuddered. Commando then. I'd find a clean pair when I got the chance. I brushed my fingers through my hair. It grazed just below my armpits. No point in putting it up. The energy would be wasted.

I breathed in deep then let it go. All right, time to face the music. Squaring my shoulders, I strode to the training room.

Two pairs of eyes flickered toward me as I entered— one brown set and the other hazel. Remy's mouth hung half open. Had I interrupted something? Elijah's face was stoic except for his intense eyes. I gulped.

"H-Hi," I said.

"Hi," Elijah replied. His tan cheeks turn slightly pink.

Silence trickled in. Remy rolled his eyes. "Welcome back. Now then. We have business to attend to."

I raised a brow. "Right now?"

"No, tomorrow." There was a pause. "Yes, right now."

"No offense Remy, but I'm in no shape or mood to do anything today. Can't we postpone for another day?"

He crossed his arms over his chest. "I have postponed it—multiple times, mind you."

I frowned. What was so important? Scratch that, if it was important then he wouldn't have put it off for so long.

"Maybe she's right," Elijah injected.

Remy turned, eyes narrowing. He pointed his finger at

Elijah's chest. "For your information, I blame you for this."

Elijah's brows shot up. "Me? What the hell did I do?"

He threw up his hands. "What haven't you done? To start with—Aislin saved you from Hell, and did you ever think to thank her?" He didn't wait for a reply. "No, of course not. You just went on your merry way. Not only that, but then you come barreling back, claiming that you were tracking Kaelin."

"I am!"

"Then next thing I know, Aislin is having a meltdown. I can only assume it was because of you—you b—"

"Not my fault. How was I supposed to know the kitsune was tracking me—much less know she was going to shatter Aislin's world?"

"You're a tracker!"

"You know, I'm right here," I intervened.

Elijah gave me an apologetic smile.

Remy continued, "Don't you have super senses? I would think you could smell her, but that's beside the point. Ever since you got here, you've been nothing but trouble."

He scoffed and ran a hand through his hair. "Trouble? Ha! All I've done is help you. I've been trying to find this Kaelin guy and you've given me nothing but shit about it. Also, it's hard to pick out a certain scent when there's a bunch of other shit around."

Remy huffed. "Sounds like more excuses to me."

Elijah threw up his hands. "Fine. Whatever, I know when I'm not wanted."

"That's not what Remy was say—"

"No, that's exactly what I'm saying." Remy waved his hand. Elijah's hands balled into fists. He shook his head and stalked out.

"Wait," I called, but he was already gone.

I turned and glared at Remy. He shrugged one shoulder. I dragged in a breath then let it out before running after him. Damn it all to Hell. I rushed to the exit. Maybe I could catch him in time. The door slammed behind me as I stopped on the sidewalk.

A gust of wind barreled into me. Strands of my hair lifted and tangoed. Fresh rain and cut grass assaulted my nose. I tilted my head up and drank in the night sky. Clouds drifted away. The stars twinkled and winked. I let it all wash over me. Goosebumps rose on my arms. The air nipped at my skin, but it was a welcome bite.

Where had the day gone? I chuckled. Right, I'd been in bed most of the day . . . or was it weeks. How long had it been? I shook my head. It didn't matter.

"Aislin."

I tensed, muscles locking up. My eyes flickered to my right then left. Nothing. Only street lights and darkness. Just my imagination. My body loosened. Voices, well one voice, in my head—nothing more. Just me—alone. I bit my lip.

"Aislin," the voice said again.

I pressed my hands to either side of my head, covering my ears. Not real. Only hearing things. I lowered my head. Without realizing, I started to rock. Was anything real? Ha, we are all puppets, but who controls the strings? No one—everyone? I bit down harder on my lip. Copper filled my mouth. At least that was real—the pain. Or was pain a figment of my imagination? My chest clenched. Chills ran up and down my body.

I closed my eyes. Was it all a dream? What if we were all dreaming or having nightmares? Did we wake up when we die? I chuckled. No, if that were true then there wouldn't be a Heaven or Hell. Yet . . . was that also a dream? Dreaming, but never waking. The Abyss of our minds.

Laughter bubbled up and left my lips. I fell to my knees. Rocks dug into my skin, but I didn't care. What were a few rocks when my world was splintering? Life was a lie, but so was death. So, then what was true? My hands slid down and rested in my lap. Nothing—nothing was true. We were living a lie, ignoring the pain and suffering of others. What was my pain compared to another?

My shoulders drooped.
"Aislin?"

I didn't move. All in my head. Maybe everything was in my head—the pain, the loss, friends. Nothing was real. Rocks crunched beside me.

"Princess?" Hands cupped my cheeks and lifted my head. Murky water.

I blinked. A tear fell. I hadn't realized I'd been crying until then.

"Are you real?" I whispered.

Chestnut brown brows furrowed. "Oh, princess." Without another word, arms pulled me up and against him.

I buried my face into his chest. Shirtless. A giggle sprung up, but soon turned into a sob. I clung to him. Rain soaked earth and autumn leaves wafted from his skin. Elijah—the knight in shining armor. His hands brushed the back of my head.

"Shh, you're okay. I got you." Elijah's arms tightened.

"I shouldn't have left."

"I'm weak," I mumbled, "I can't do anything right."

He chuckled. His chest vibrated under my ear. I leaned back, lips puckered and brow pulled down.

"You're not weak, princess." I raised a brow, tilting my head. "You're not. You're a lot stronger than you give yourself credit for, believe me. And if anybody has the right to say they can't do anything right," he puffed up his chest,

"that would be me."

The corners of my lips curved upwards. He grinned.

"Atta girl. Show that pretty smile."

I ducked my head, smile widening. I bit the side of my lip. "Thanks."

"Any time, princess." He reached out and tucked a strand of hair behind my ear.

His finger grazed against my cheek. I sucked in a breath. My eyes flicked up to his. The stars danced in his now green eyes. I opened my mouth then closed it again. Elijah's gaze dropped to my lips then back. I gulped.

My heart drummed in my ears. I could only assume he heard it too. As if in answer, his lips tilted up on one side.

He leaned in.

"Aislin!" Ignore it. I tilted my head to the right.

His fingers brushed against my right cheek before settling there completely. I leaned into it.

"God damn it, Aislin, listen to me!" I jerked. Not real— only in my head.

Elijah paused, brows cinching together.

"Not here—not now," I mumbled.

"Princess?" He questioned at the same time the voice screamed, *"Aislin, you're in danger!"*

I stumbled backwards. My hands covered my ears. Elijah's eyes narrowed, body tensing. I shook my head over and over. This wasn't happening—not again.

"Stop it," I rocked. "this isn't real. You're not real."

Elijah put a hand on my shoulder. I flinched. His hand fell to his side.

"Tell me what's wrong, princess, so I can help."

I laughed, lifting my gaze. "Help? You can't help crazy."

He frowned. "You're not crazy."

My fingers dug into my hair. "I'm hearing voices, Elijah. Most people would call that crazy." I sighed, licking my lips. "I'm losing my mind—just like Kaydynce's mom."

"Who?"

"Doesn't matter. I'm falling without a safety net— nothing to catch me."

"I won't let you fall," he growled, cupping my cheek again.

I smiled weakly. "Too late."

"It's never too late." His lips captured mine.

Chapter 21

I fell. I fell into the brackish water and into his hungry lips. He groaned and pulled me closer. My body went limp in his arms. Heat coursed up my skin. I kissed him back with the same insistence. Elijah's fingers dug into my hips. I bit back a moan. How long had it been since someone kissed me like this? My chest tightened. Kaelin.

I broke away. My breath came in ragged gasps. Elijah didn't loosen his grip. He too was breathing fast.

"Wow," he breathed.

I lifted my hand to my lips. Tender to the touch. Guilt washed over me. "I-I shouldn't have done that."

Elijah chuckled and pulled me closer. "Done what?" He whispered, leaning in. "Kiss me?"

I nodded, cheeks on fire. My lashes covered my eyes. "I wasn't thinking."

He rolled his eyes, smirking. "That's the point, princess. Act on emotion—don't think, just do."

I sighed, and nuzzled into his arms. I knew I should have pulled away, but the heat from his skin warmed the chill running down my body.

"That's precisely the problem. I don't act on anything—much less emotion. Think and plan—that's my system."

Elijah snorted. "Well, your system needs an update."

It was my turn to roll my eyes. "My system is just fine, thank you."

He raised his hands, rearing back. "All right, whatever you say, princess."

His hands glided down to my waist again. I shivered despite the warmth of his touch.

"So . . . are you still leaving?"

Elijah's brows shot up. "Leave? Now? After that kiss?" he laughed, deep and throaty. "Fuck no." His smirk widened, eyes dancing. "I'm here to stay." His smile faltered. "That is, if you'll have me."

My heart clenched. I turned my head, and closed my eyes for a moment. Did I want him to stay? Different emotions fought for number one. Everything was happening so fast, yet at the same time, too slow. I wasn't sure what I wanted— much less what was real. His hands fell to his sides. He took a step back. Crestfallen.

"I see."

My eyes snapped up to his face. All the light, playfulness disappeared. A mask covered the emotions.

"I . . . it's just . . ."

"No, I get it. Don't worry, Aislin." I winced at the use of my name. "It's my fault. I should have known better."

"Elijah, please don't be upset."

He turned his back to me and ran a hand through his hair. "Ha. Who says I'm upset? It's not like I opened myself up to you, and what do you do?" He gazed back, pain in his murky eyes. "You stomp all over me."

Heat snaked up my body. I ground my teeth. "You knew I was looking for Kaelin. Did you ever think of the reason why?"

He swiveled around, hazel eyes blazing. "It's been almost two fucking years, Aislin! Most people would have moved on by now."

My hands balled into fists. "I'm not like most people!"

Elijah laughed—cold and harsh. "Yeah, I see that. You're mentally unstable—maybe that's why you haven't moved on. Most people are sane." I gasped, my eyes widening. He winced. "I-I didn't mean it like that."

I shook my head, stumbling backwards. Tears threatened to fall. Pain ripped through my chest.

"I-If you didn't mean it...you wouldn't have said it."

"That's not true." He reached out a hand, but pulled it back. "It's just, ugh, frustrating. One minute your walls are down and we are kissing, then next thing I know you're pulling away with your walls in place again." His hand ran down his face, stretching the skin.

I bit my lip. "I-I'm sorry."

He let out a deep breath. His murky water eyes searched mine. "If you weren't ready or God forbid, didn't want this, then you should have said something."

I sniffled. "What was I supposed to say? Oh, I'm sorry, but I'm still hung up on my first love—the boy I couldn't save from what I am."

"Shit. Well, that explains some of it."
I frowned. "What do you mean?"

Elijah's lips lifted slightly, brows crinkling. "You can't move on because you blame yourself for his death. The only way you can ever be happy is if you forgive yourself." He cast his eyes down. "It wasn't your fault. There wasn't anything you could have done to save him."

"You're wrong." Tears streamed down my cheeks. "I saw his death. The curse of a banshee—seeing the deaths of the ones they love. If only I had gotten there sooner, he wouldn't be gone."

Elijah strode the distance and pulled me against him. My head rested over his pounding heart. His hand brushed down my hair. The tears intensified. My body quivered, racked with choked out sobs.

"Shh, there was nothing you could have done, princess. If it was his time, then he would have died either way. You can't keep blaming yourself for something you had no control over."

"I just . . . I don't want to lose anyone else."

His arms tightened around me. The hand in my hair balled up. "That's not up to you. That's part of life—death. There's a reason for everything."

I lifted my head and stared into his eyes. "Do you really believe that?"

He smiled. "Yes, I do. Why else would I be here?"

I shook my head. I didn't have an answer. Was it fate or destiny? Did that even exist? Too many questions, not enough answers.

"Life is a mystery," I mumbled.

He chuckled, eyes brightening. "Exactly, princess. So, go out there and live it—explore and discover."

The corners of my lips curved up. "You make it sound so easy."

"It's only as easy as you make it."

I tilted my head to the left. My hair shifted to match the movement. "When did you become so smart?"

He flashed his pearly whites. "When I was born."
I giggled. "What a big ego you have."

He chuckled. "The better to sweep you off your feet with." His fingers grazed my cheek. I closed my eyes.

Forgive myself. Could I wash away all my sins? The death of Kaelin, and countless others I'd killed. Could I be happy? I smiled and opened my eyes. Maybe. Don't think, just do.

I brought my hand up and cupped his cheek. Elijah's hazel eyes widened. My smile broadened. I leaned in and placed my lips against his. Act on emotion. I wanted to be happy, if he could give it to me, then I'd concede.

Chapter 22

Kaydynce

"The time is finally upon us," Illium said, buttoning up his shirt.

I groaned, rolling over onto my stomach. The blankets tangled around my legs. "Is it that important?"

Illium leaned in close. The bed dipped slightly. He trailed a finger under my chin. I fluttered my eyelashes, my lips curving up.

"That depends, sweetheart. Do you think taking over the Human Realm is unimportant?"

I rolled my eyes and twirled a strand of hair around my finger. "Well, of course not. I just don't understand why now."

Illium flicked my chin up, indigo eyes bright. "Why not?" He opened his arms out wide and encompassed the whole room. "Today is as good of a day as any other."

My lower lip jutted out. "I know, it's just . . . do you have to go with them?"

He chuckled. "Now what kind of king would I be if I didn't join my people in war?"

"A live one," I mumbled. The Death Call still rang in my head despite the months that had passed.

Betrayal and death. I shivered.

Illium clucked his tongue. "Now now, I'm not going to die. If I do, however," his eyes shifted violet, "I'm going to take down as many humans as I possibly can."

A grin spread across my lips. "Oh, I don't doubt that. It's just," I nibbled on my lower lip, "if you go, I want to go too."

He sighed and sat on the side of the bed. "You know it wouldn't be safe for you out there. Remember what happened last time." His fingers travelled down my shoulder. "I'd hate for you to encounter Aislin again, especially after what she tried to do to you."

Ha, what she tried to do to me was nothing. That's not what I'd told him, though. Poor Kaydynce, the little queen, couldn't protect herself from a banshee. I was the victim. The people had rallied around me. Some had cried for blood. No one hurt the queen. The corners of my lips lifted. Barely a finger raised, and they were fighting for me.

"Don't worry my love, with all of the creatures we've riled up, we can't lose."

My grin faltered. Uncertainty rose. Could we really do this? "The Human Realm is so vast. How can we possibly conquer it all?"

"Have faith. We need not conquer it all—not at first at least. We will take city by city—rallying any supernatural being that chooses to join the cause."

I let out my breath. He had a plan. I shuffled closer to him and rested my chin on his lap. Faith. It wasn't something I trusted.

"I trust you," I said without thinking.

Illium raised a brow, the corners of his lips curving upwards. "You shouldn't."

If it was anybody else, I would have been worried. Yet it was different with Illium. Elves were known for twisting the truth and tricking the person too stupid to read between the lines. I knew the game.

"Just come back to me, okay?"

"As my queen wishes." I nodded and nuzzled his thigh.

As long as he came back to me, that's all that mattered. The Death Call would never happen. I just wished he didn't have to go.

"Stay with me a little bit longer," I begged, running a hand down his hip.

"I cannot, my love. So much to do, so little time."

I straightened and crossed my arms over my chest. "You are the king. Have someone else make the plans and enforce them. We have enough subjects who would do that without a second thought."

Illium's eyes narrowed. "You expect me to hand off my responsibilities to someone else, who I assume will be unfit for the task?" He shook his head, white blonde hair tumbled over his shoulders. "No, I cannot."

I flicked my hair off my shoulder. "Fine then. Just go since that's what you seem to want. So go have your stupid war. When you leave, send in one of the guards—preferably the handsome one."

The temperature in the room dropped. Ice formed on the doorframe. I shivered, the hairs on my arms rising.

"I will do no such thing."

I threw my hands into the air. "Fine. I guess you expect me to be bored the whole time you're gone."

He sighed and put a hand over his eyes. "Explore the Other Realm if you choose. I doubt anything I say will dissuade you from doing whatever you decide."

"Damn right," I said, folding my arms again.

His hand fell away from his face. Some emotion hid behind his indigo eyes, but I didn't know what. He pursed his lips.

"Very well." Illium got up and bowed. "Then I shall take my leave, my queen. If you have a need for me, I shall be in my study."

I nodded, hands crumbling into my lap. He held my gaze for a moment before swiveling on his heels and left. I watched him go. There was nothing I could do to stop him.

He would do what he wanted—like me. My fingers curled around the blanket and pulled it to my chin. There was nothing to worry about.

The words didn't comfort me. I sucked in a breath and let it out. My grip tightened on the blanket before I flung it off. Goosebumps rose on my naked body. I glanced at the open door. Nothing moved. Where was everyone? I shook my head. The study, of course. I should probably get dressed. A naked queen was a distraction, and I doubted Illium would appreciate it either.

But what to wear? Something simple, yet an attention grabber. My feet touched the stone floor. The cold radiated through my soles. I shivered. That was one thing I hadn't gotten used to—the cold. The unworldly frigidness. In the Human Realm, it barely phased me, yet here was different.

I sauntered to the mahogany wardrobe in the corner. Leaves were etched into the wood, creating intricate vine works. I pulled open the double doors and scanned the array of dresses. Blue ones, purple ones, some yellow and green, others with floral designs—nothing popped out. A growl bubbled up. Was there nothing cute in here? I reached for a deep burgundy one all the way in the back.

I held it out in front of me. Sweetheart neckline and form-fitted. Not a bad choice. The dress's sleeves fell off the shoulders in strips around the arms. I pressed it against my body, examining how it would fit. The hem came just above my mid-thigh in the front except for a small strip of fabric in the middle. The corners of my lips twisted upwards.

Perfect.

It didn't take long for me to slip into the dress. The material clung to my body like a second skin. My hands glided down my tiny waist and hips. Now I was ready. My eyes flickered to the vanity across the room. The mirror reflected my image: shoulder-length blonde hair, sapphire blue eyes, and pale complexion. I frowned.

I needed a focal point, other than my figure. My eyes landed on a small cylinder. Ah ha. Lipstick was what I needed. My feet skipped toward it. I snatched it up and grinned. Bright red. The perfect color. I glanced in the mirror and smirked. Onward to the study. I'd be damned if I wasn't included.

The walk out the room and through the hallway was quiet. A hush had fallen over the castle. Barely contained excitement bubbled just under the surface. Energy hissed and crackled in the air. Strands of hair rose.

I brushed them down and sauntered passed the entry way and dining hall. The study was in the back of the castle, up a spiraling staircase, and to the right—away from prying eyes and windows.

My bare feet made no noise as I approached. A heavy, leaf engraved door stood between me and Illium. I straightened my shoulders and lifted my chin before throwing open the door.

Six pairs of eyes snapped up and met my gaze. Only one set didn't—Illium's.

"Was there something you needed, my queen?" He asked, flipping through papers.

He didn't even look at me. I stormed to the end of the table. Three creatures sat on either side of the oval table. Illium sat at the head.

"I demand to be included in this."

His violet eyes lifted. I straightened even more under his stare. "Have I proclaimed you may not do such a thing?"

I fidgeted. "This is my war too—my people."

Illium's lips curved up on one side. "You may join the discussion, my queen. I would never decree you couldn't, but joining in the fight is a different matter."

I ground my teeth. Elf logic. "I want to fight alongside my people. I too have a responsibility to keep."

His eyes flashed. "You demand to be included in this, which I am doing. You have yet to specify what you would like to be included in."

Ugh! "The fight, damn it! How many times must I tell you this?"

Silence filled the room. Eyes shifted from one another. Words whispered. Illium pushed himself up slowly. I gulped but held my head up higher. Chills ran up and down my back.

"That is no way to talk to your king." His voice was low and stern. My heart pounded against my chest.

Bow to him. My hands clenched at my sides. The urge to beg forgiveness coated my throat. *Fight it, Kaydynce.* My jaw locked up. The whispers grew louder. Every part of me tensed. I wouldn't break.

His eyes narrowed. "Very well." He flicked his chin at the silver-haired elf to his right. "Take the queen back to her quarters."

The elf nodded and got up. His chair scraped against the floor. I winced. My pulse skyrocketed. *Run. Run,* I told myself, but my legs didn't move. I was frozen to the spot. Ice clamped around my feet. The chill spread upwards. I gasped, my wide eyes finding violet ones. Anger simmered just underneath. I gulped, bile rising.

"Please follow me, my queen," the elf said, grabbing my arm.

I snatched it away. "I know where my quarters are." I turned my gaze to the elf. "But I wouldn't mind you joining me."

His pale cheeks flushed pink. I grinned. No persuasion needed. I spun on my heels, the ice vanishing, and strode out. The elf followed close behind.

Chapter 23

Aislin

"Do you think we should tell him?" Elijah asked as he came up behind me.

I shook my head. "No reason to. It's not like its important information anyways. I think it would be best if we forgot it ever happened."

"You say that," his hand grazed my back, and I shivered. "But I know you don't mean it. Why else would it happen, if you didn't want it to?"

I turned and glared. "That's not the point."
He raised a brow. "Isn't it though?"

I rolled my eyes. His lips curved into a lop-sided grin.
"We don't tell him."
"Tell who, what?" Remy asked, walking from the shower room.

A towel was slung around his neck and his glasses were slightly fogged.

"Um, don't tell, um," I struggled for an excuse.
Elijah sighed. "It's my birthday."

My mouth fell open, but I closed it quickly. "Right. We didn't think it was important," I shot Elijah a look. He grinned, "since we have a lot of stuff going on already."

Remy narrowed his eyes, but didn't question it. "Aislin is quite right. Happy birthday, but we have other matters to attend to. Like, for example, the possibility of war and enslavement."

"What did you just say?" Elijah asked. I glanced at him, meeting murky eyes.

Remy pulled the towel off his neck. "My sources have heard a rumor of war and the enslavement of humanity."

"I remember you saying something like that a while back, but I thought it was just a rumor. Do you really think it's possible?" Uneasiness settled in the pit of my stomach.

Remy frowned. "Anything is possible. Who knows how many supernatural beings are in this city, much less the whole world? I can only assume most of them are Esor Animi— soul eaters—since they would be the ones who would reap the benefits."

"Okay, so what do we do? Do we have a plan?" Remy shook his head. "Anything?" Elijah ran a hand through his hair.

"I've been trying for months to come up with a plan of action," Remy's shoulders sagged, "but nothing. I searched through every spell I knew, but nothing popped up."

I bit my lip. There was only one option left. "Let's meet them head-on."

"What!?" Remy and Elijah said at the same time.

"Are you crazy, princess? Look around!" Elijah raised his arms and stretched them out. "We have no army. Three people don't stand a chance against who knows how many."

I crossed my arms over my chest. "I know that, but what other option do we have?"

"Join them."

I spun around to face him. "Now who's the crazy one?"

Elijah shrugged. "You asked what other options we had and I gave you one. I'm not saying to do that, I'm just putting it out there."

"Yeah, thanks for the contribution," I muttered sarcastically.

He grinned, hazel eyes dancing. "Any time, princess."

A cough snapped our attention back to Remy. I took a step back, creating a bit of distance between us. A low growl emanated from Elijah. I shot him a glare before focusing on Remy again.

"Is something going on between you two?"

"No—"

"—Yes," Elijah interjected.

I sighed, pressing a hand to my forehead. "No, nothing is going on," I narrowed my eyes, "between us."

Elijah smirked, but kept his mouth shut. Remy shook his head.

"You're a horrible liar, but we'll discuss that later. Right now, we need to focus on the problem at hand. Joining them isn't an option, not unless you want a quicker death. But meeting them head on wouldn't be a good idea either."

"Okay, do you think there is any way we can dissuade them from attacking?"

"Better question," Elijah said, "who is launching this attack?"

Remy didn't have to answer. I knew exactly who.

"Illium," I said.

Elijah reared back, eyebrows raised. "Why would Illium want to do that? Don't get me wrong, I can see that piece of shit doing something like this, but it requires planning and a hell of a lot of recruiting."

My whole body drooped. My heart plummeted. "Kaydynce. She must have been doing the recruiting—using her powers."

Elijah frowned. "Last I heard, she had a near-death experience and couldn't leave the kingdom. So how could she recruit anyone if she's stuck in the Other Realm?"

My brows creased. "Near-death experience?" My eyes widened. "Shit."

"What? Elijah asked.

I sagged against the doorframe. Was this because of me? No, we had heard about it way before then, but still. She wouldn't, would she?

"I think some of this might be my fault."

"How the hell is it your fault, princess? It's not like you did something to upset him or anything." I ducked my head. His mouth formed an O. "*You* were the near-death experience, which means . . . you tried to kill the queen!"

My head snapped up. "Woah, just wait one minute," I held up my hands. "I didn't try to kill her. *She* attacked *me*. I was just defending myself, but I didn't hurt her." I paused. "I didn't get the chance to." Elijah snarled. "She had a Death Call, okay? That was her near-death, though they usually are the death of the one you love." But who did Kaydynce love? Illium? I laughed.

Both Remy and Elijah glared at me. "This isn't a laughing matter, Aislin."

I covered my mouth. "Sorry, just had a funny thought is all."

"Mhmm, so the real question is—can we stop them before they get here?" Remy asked, pushing up his glasses.

"Would we be able to teleport to the Other Realm instead?" Elijah asked, glancing between the two of us.

I focused my attention on Remy. "I don't know. Do you think that's possible?"

His brows creased. "If by teleport you mean open a doorway, possibly. I'd have to go back over my spell book first. I might have missed something."

I nodded, picking myself up. "All right. How long do you think that would take?"

"It's hard to say at this point. Go wash up and nap. I'll let you know when I have something more concrete."

"Thanks. I doubt I need either, though food would be appreciated." To emphasize my point, my stomach gurgled and grumbled.

Remy rolled his eyes. "All right then, go eat. I'll be in the study." Without another word, he turned and walked off.

Elijah peeked into the hallway then turned back with a wink. "We're alone once again."

I giggled, shaking my head. "Perv."

He shrugged and snaked an arm around my waist. "I can be whatever you want me to be, princess."

"Noted." I dragged a finger down his five o' clock shadow.

He closed his eyes for a second. When he opened them again, they burned a forest green. I sucked in a breath. My pulse spiked. A grin spread across his lips. "Food first . . . then whatever comes next." I nodded and pushed open the door.

~ ~ ~

An hour passed without anything to report. Remy stayed in the study. There was no point in disturbing him. I sighed, running my fingers through my hair.

"How long can it take to find a stupid spell?"

"Um, as long as it takes. It wouldn't be simple to find either. I just hope we make it in time," I said, resting my elbows on my knees.

"Don't worry, princess, war takes time, and if Illium is smart he'll plan every little detail and possible slipup."

He was right, I knew that, but doubt still crept in. Who knew what would happen if or when we got there. There was no way of telling until we entered the Other Realm. I closed my eyes and rested my head in my hands.

"Found it!"

My head snapped up. Elijah held out a hand. I took it without question. He pulled me to my feet. His hand cupped my cheek as he leaned in. My lips found his. Emotion surged up. My arms wrapped around his neck. He deepened the kiss, his lips insistent, then it was over.

Green eyes danced. "Just in case," he whispered before following Remy's voice.

I stood there for a moment and watched his retreating form. Just in case of what? The likelihood of death? I closed my eyes. Death was no stranger to me.

The best I could hope for would be a quick death. My hands fell to my stomach. The wound still pained me. I'd almost died at the hands of Kaelin's killer, yet Remy had saved me. The swish and slurp of the Leaf Blade as it gouged my abdomen would forever haunt me.

I ran a hand down the right side of my face. This was it. Stopping Illium was the only option. I won't allow the human race to be enslaved. The horrors the world would see. Death would be merciful compared to what the supernatural creatures would do to them. I sighed, squared my shoulders, and followed Elijah into Remy's study.

Remy stood over his desk, glasses hanging from the tip of his nose.

"You said you found something," I said, pushing past Elijah.

Remy nodded, his glasses falling off his nose only to hang by his ears. He pushed them back into place.

"Yes, I think there might be a way to open a portal, but we would be detected immediately."

I pursed my lips. "That's a chance we are going to have to take."

"Not necessarily." Elijah leaned against the doorframe, arms crossed over his chest.

My right brow lifted. "Oh? Do tell, how would we avoid it?"

His lips curved up. "Send me first. I doubt they would suspect anything from me."

"Ha! Do you think Illium would be that stupid?" I shook my head. "It wouldn't work. You've been with us for a month or two already. My guess is, he would immediately suspect an ambush."

"She does have a point," Remy said.

"Then what's the plan?" Elijah asked, pushing off the frame.

"We portal to the Other Realm, into the castle if possible, and go from there."

Elijah slapped a hand to his face then dragged it down.

"That's all you got, princess? No offense, but that's suicide."

I put my hands on my hips. "I don't see you coming up with anything of use, Mr. Don't Think, Just Do."

He stalked toward me. "We are charging headlong to our deaths. I don't know if you realize that, but just going from there doesn't help. I'd rather go out swinging with a plan of action."

I stood my ground. "Oh, I'm sorry, but I have no idea what this castle looks like. So, it's a little bit harder to form a plan when I don't know what I'm doing!"

"Yeah, I can see that."

I ground my teeth. "You aren't doing much better!"

"Enough!" Remy slammed his hands down on the desk. I jumped, heart in my throat. "This is not the time for a lover's quarrel. So, if you two are done," we both nodded, "then I'd like to propose another option." I opened my mouth. He raised a hand. I closed it. "Portaling into the castle, as you said Elijah, is suicide, but if we portal close enough, we might be able to sneak in undetected."

I bit my lip. It wasn't that bad of a plan. It would also give us a little bit more time to think it all through. Come up with a better plan later.

"Let's do it."

Elijah's lips turned down, and his hazel eyes narrowed. "You mean like, right now?"

I shrugged. "Why not? The sooner the better." I cast a look to Remy.

He settled down into his chair again. His fingers bridged together as he leaned back in the seat.

"I don't see why not."

I swung to face Elijah. "Ha!"

Elijah rolled his eyes, a grin spreading across his face.

"Yeah, yeah, whatever, princess."

"So, what do we need to do?" I asked, glancing around the room.

"Well, I'll cast the spell and a doorway, much like the one Illium uses, will appear. The tricky part, though, is for it to work, we all have to imagine the place we want to go."

"Which is difficult because only one of us has ever been there," I finished.

"Precisely."

Elijah smirked. "Now who's laughing? Oh wait, that's me. And who is the only one who's been to the Other Realm? Ha, guess what, that's me yet again."

"Ass," I mumbled, but a bit louder I said, "Okay, so how do we get around that?"

"Easy. I cast the spell," Elijah said, putting his hands behind his head.

My brows flew up. "You can't be serious."

His grin widened. "Oh, I'm dead serious, princess."

My nostrils flared and my eyes narrowed. "No offense, Elijah, but for a spell to work you need to be a wizard and that you are not."

"Well, actually," I groaned, knowing exactly where this was going. "I don't see why he couldn't if he knew the spell."

"Ugh, fine, you win," I sneered. Elijah chuckled.

"Oh, what did you say? I couldn't hear you—can you repeat that?"

I rolled my eyes. "I'm not saying it again." I turned to Remy. "So, the spell—any ingredients needed?"

"Nope, just words."

"Okay, then let's get on with it."

~ ~ ~

Three tries—it took three damn tries for the portal to open. A bluish doorway manifested out of thin air.

"Finally," I groaned, wiping the hair from my face.

"Oh, shut up. At least I got it to open," Elijah snapped, hazel eyes narrowing.

"Yeah, I should hope so after three tries. So now what? Do we just walk through or what?"

Remy pushed himself up and examined the doorway with the spell book in hand. "If Elijah pictured the right place, then yes, we should be able to just walk through with no problem."

He flipped through the book, glasses falling to the bridge of his nose. A frown marred his lips.

"Wait, I might have found something else," he said, finger skimming over one of the pages.

"Please, tell me it's good news." I stared at the doorway inches away from Elijah and me, its bluish light casting an eerie glow on the room.

"Um, I may have translated the text incorrectly."

I threw my hands into the air. "God damn it, Remy."

His ebony cheeks flushed a light pink. "It's not the easiest language to read, you know."

"Go easy on the kid, princess, he's trying his best."

I gaped at Elijah. Remy's brown eyes narrowed as he pushed up his glasses. He slammed the book shut with one hand. Oh, shit. This wasn't good.

"I am not a kid. I am older than you think, so I would appreciate it if you treated me as such."

Elijah's lips lifted, his eyes brightened. "All right, old man."

I snorted. Remy turned his glare my way. I covered my mouth. Oops.

"The text actually reads," he said through clenched teeth, "the one who enters must think of the place they want to go—just not in so many words."

"That's you, big boy," I said, gesturing to Elijah, "so, go ahead, walk through that door."

Elijah made no move toward it. I raised a brow. He stood in front of the doorway, hands motionless at his sides.

"Elijah?" No response. I bit my lip and placed a hand on his shoulder.

He whirled and grabbed my wrist. I yelped. A deep growl sent chills down my spine. Yellow-green eyes held my wide-eyed gaze. I froze. My heart jumped to my throat. Elijah bared slightly elongated teeth. His grip tightened on my wrist. I winced, holding back a whimper. Remy moved to intervene. I held up my other hand. There was no point in doing more damage than good, which would have happened if he moved any closer to a very alert werewolf.

"E-Elijah," I stuttered, "it's me, p-princess. Remember?" His growl receded. I let out a breath.

He blinked. His eyes shifted to murky waters again. "P-Princess?"

I nodded, shoulders relaxing. He glanced at the hand on my wrist and dropped it like he'd been burned. Remy straightened behind him, relief showing on his face. At least I wasn't the only one worried. "Hi."

He grinned. "Hi, back."

"Time is of the essence. This door won't stay open for long, so I suggest if we plan on doing this, we need to get a move on."

"Right." I motioned to Elijah. "You must go in first, and remember to think of the place we are going."

His brow creased. "Wait, what?"

"The Other World—picture it in your mind then walk through. We'll be right behind you."

He nodded, closed his eyes, and strode through. The light sucked him in without a problem. I inhaled and let it out. I glanced at Remy. He nodded. My eyes took in the room once more. Bookshelves lined the walls, dust coating everything. Would I be coming back here at all? I wasn't sure, but if I went out fighting, I'd be okay. Taking another deep breath, I walked through the archway.

Chapter 24

Kaydynce

Warmth spread through my body. I relished in it. When was the last time I'd felt anything other than cold? My lips curved up. Blue electricity skidded off my skin and across his. Silver hair pulled back into a ponytail that fell just shy of his waist. What was his name? I shook my head. It didn't matter. He was but a toy, and Illium knew that. Why else would he ask this boy to escort me back to my chambers?

Anger was fleeting and Illium knew as well as I did about the mood swings of a hungry succubus. I licked my lips. Vanilla and licorice. Each being tasted different. Some were sweet, others were savory with a kick. The gnawing hunger sated for the moment, I dropped my hand from his face. He blinked, his silver eyes focusing again.

"M-My queen, what . . ." he glanced around, cheeks flushing. "Please forgive me."

I chuckled. "No forgiveness needed. Though stay close, I may need you soon."

He bowed, taking a step back. "Yes, my queen."

I leaned my head against the wall. The burning cold touch was enough to ignite a need in me. It wasn't just the hunger. A sexual need had reared its head. It wouldn't be hard to persuade the poor boy. One touch and he'd be mine—like so many others.

"If you don't mind me asking, what is it you are called?"

His eyes widened, mouth falling open. "Um, Oakland, my queen."

I nodded. "Oakland, do you think I'm pretty?"

"I-I shouldn't." His cheeks flushed even more. I stepped forward and pressed a hand to his chest. "Y-yes, my queen. You are more than pretty. You are the sun that rises in the sky."

My lips curved up. I giggled. "How poetic."

He ducked his head. My fingers travelled up and down his chest. He shivered. Pain licked up my stomach. Hunger beat at my door once more. My hand balled in his shirt. All I had to do was pull his lips to mine and it would be over.

Restraint. It was something I'd been working on. Trying not to kill when I fed. Each taste would be sweeter if I only nibbled at times. I sighed, releasing him and pushing off the wall.

"My queen?"

I ignored him and sauntered passed. Oakland followed on my heels. I smirked. Good dog. Now where to? I closed my eyes. My lips tilted down. Oakland hadn't been enough. I needed something a bit stronger. Illium.

I bit my lip. Would he still be in the study? There was only one way to find out. Need crashed into me. I stumbled. The hunger was like a punch to the stomach. My arms wrapped around my abdomen.

I whimpered. Why was it so strong? It wasn't like I hadn't just fed. Was his life-force so weak that it barely did anything?

"My queen!" Oakland's arms wrapped around my shoulder. "What is it? Are you hurt?"

I shook my head. My hand grabbed his. "Find Illium."

"I-I can't just leave you here, my queen."

My fingers danced under his palm. Blue energy surged and swirled. "Please, Oakland, go find Illium and bring him to me."

"Yes, my queen, as you wish." He slinked off. I sighed and stumbled over to the closest wall.

I leaned my head against it and closed my eyes. The world spun and tilted. I opened my eyes. Nothing changed. The stone walls swayed and slanted. The gnawing pain intensified. I let out a cry, curling up into a ball.

Dark spots flickered in and out of my vision. I blinked. This wasn't normal. Had he poisoned me? I frowned. If that was so, then why? I scoffed at the idea. No, that wasn't possible. No one would be that stupid.

My chest tightened. An insistent throb spread through my head. I gritted my teeth. Where was Illium? Pain stabbed through my cranium. I screamed. Darkness took over. Everything around me vanished, all but the vision. My second Death Call. The clash of metal, the ripping of flesh— violence and blood, so much blood. The death played like a film wheel. His death—Illium.

I sucked in a shaky breath as the vision faded. Tears trailed down my cheeks, leaving a wet path. Pain radiated up my legs. I winced and glanced down. My knees popped as I shifted. When had I fallen?

I closed my eyes and rested my throbbing head against the wall. Involuntary motion. The vision, the fall to my knees—it didn't matter. Death. Death was approaching.

I fumbled up, legs wobbly. I leaned against the wall to steady myself. My stomach knotted and churned.

"Intruders!" someone yelled.

I froze, muscles locking up. My pulse quickened. The vision flashed through my mind. Guards charged by without a single glance my way. Purple and blue clothes blurred. The world spun. Illium! My body snapped into action. I stumbled forward and took off. He couldn't die—not by her. I barreled by creatures of all kinds in similar purple and blue uniforms.

Sideward glances and glares, but I didn't care. All that mattered was preventing Illium's death. My heels clicked on the stone floor, echoing off the walls. Hallway after hallway with no sign of him. My eyes flickered every which way, hoping to catch a glimpse of white-blonde hair.

I skidded to a halt at the archway to the main entrance. There he was. My heart sped up. Blonde hair pulled back into a low ponytail, a deep purple shirt unbuttoned at the top, and cold indigo eyes. I shivered. My eyes drunk him in then paused, following his gaze. Everything inside stilled.

She was here. Aislin.

Chapter 25

Elijah

Think where you want to go. Easy. The problem was, I didn't want to go back to the Other World. Focus. My heart kicked and punched my chest. I closed my eyes and took a deep breath. Aislin shifted beside me, but I ignored her. Focus.

Grass waving in the warm breeze, the stone castle towering over everything, the small riverbed trickling from the stone pathway and down into the jungle of the Other World. I could see it all right before my very eyes. Home. I never thought I'd ever go back.

The Other World was different from any place I'd ever been. Pleasant temperatures, the occasional drizzle, and any creature imaginable. Some considered it a paradise, others called it a hell hole. It was both. I'd left it for a reason, like so many others.

A hand touched my shoulder. Instinct took over. I swiveled around, snatching the person's wrist in my hands. A deep rumble shook through my chest. I stared into wide blue eyes. Long auburn hair fell around her shoulders.

Her supple lips moved, but I didn't catch the words. Honeysuckle and summer breeze drifted up my nostrils. I blinked, shaking off the wolf.

"P-Princess?" Relax. The muscles in my back unwound.

She nodded. I glanced at my hand on her wrist and let go quickly.

"Hi."

A grin spread across my lips. "Hi, back." I fell into the sea of her eyes. I fought the urge to brush back her hair.

"Time is of the essence. This door won't stay open for long, so I suggest if we plan on doing this, we need to get a move on," Remy said.

"Right." Aislin motioned to me. "You must go in first, and remember to think of the place we are going."

My brow creased. "Wait, what?" What was I getting myself into?

"The Other World—picture it in your mind then walk through. We'll be right behind you."

I nodded, closed my eyes, and strode through. *Picture where you want to go.* Energy sizzled in the confines of whatever this place was. The hairs on my arms snapped up. My eyes opened. Darkness surrounded me. Silence. Eerie silence.

There was no noise—no footsteps, no birds chirping or whatever, and no sign of life other than the pounding of my heart. The stench of fear clogged my senses. I gulped. The pitch blackness went on and on. I ground my teeth. This was getting me nowhere!

My hands balled into fists at my sides. March to our deaths. Fight for humanity. I shook my head. No, fight for the ones who can't. That's why I was doing this, right? I sighed and rand a hand through my already tousled hair. Aislin would be following close behind, so why couldn't I hear her or catch the soft whiff of honeysuckle? I flexed my hands and kept walking.

Picture where you want to go, they said. Piece of cake. Only it wasn't. I let out a deep breath and let go of all other thoughts rolling around in my head. This was not the time to think of soft lips against mine or the lightest of touches as her hands fluttered to my cheeks. Focus. The Other World.

Where it all began—my birth and rebirth.

I closed my eyes again. Grass whipping against my ankles, the gurgles of the rapids in the distance, a castle of old stone and as high as the sky. A buzz picked up in volume. My eyes snapped open. A bluish-white doorway stood a foot or two away. My heart skipped a beat. There it was—the exit. I picked up the pace. The light intensified the closer I got. I shielded my eyes as I stepped through the portal.

Sunlight beamed down, warming my skin. I tensed, glancing around at my surroundings. Bright green grass swayed in a gentle breeze. Roses drifted on the wind. Well, this seemed right. I lifted my nose, breathing in the different scents. Sandy river banks, more roses, and the subtle hint of mossy rocks. Fresh air with none of the pollution found in the Human Realm. The castle towered over me.

Grey stone created a fortress of protection. An air current tickled my skin and lifted my shirt. A grin spread across my lips. I tilted my head back and to my right. Open space. A castle on a cliff. Birds chirped and cawed in the distance. A rocky cliffside with roaring rapids beneath. Water bubbled and splashed, sending a spray of fresh water into the air. Droplets splattered my skin. Cool and refreshing.

Energy sizzled and crackled around me. The hair on my arms rose. My heart jumped. I glanced beside me. A shimmering white door appeared, flickering in and out of focus. My nostrils flared, muscles tensing up more.

Honeysuckle and the sweet aroma of a summer breeze drifted through the doorway. I relaxed, letting out the breath

I held. A grin spread across my lips as Aislin stumbled out, tripping over her own feet. Remy followed close behind. My eyes roamed over her. Every red-brown strand of hair out of place, her pale skin, and eyes as bright as the water below. I gulped.

"Took you long enough. I was beginning to worry." Aislin rolled her eyes, pink lips curving upwards. "Whatever. So what's the plan?"

I frowned. Was I supposed to come up with the plan? Fuck. I rubbed a hand behind my head.

"Um, hide? I can only assume a guard or something will be patrolling this area at some point."

Aislin nodded, her hair bounced with her movement. I watched, mesmerized. My hands itched to run through it and balled it up into my fists.

"Right." She glanced around, lips tilting down. "Um, where exactly?"

I sighed, cupping the back of my head. "The only place we can—the castle."

Remy raised a brow. "Wouldn't that set off some sort of alarm?"

I shrugged. "Probably, but that was the plan to begin with, right? Face them head on."

Remy pressed his thumb and index fingers on the bridge of his nose.

"Is that the best you got?" Aislin asked, crossing her arms over her chest.

"Why, yes, it is," I bowed, extending my right arm, "unless it pleases you otherwise, princess."

She narrowed her blue eyes. "No, it's fine. Head on, perfect." I smirked "I assume you expect us to just waltz right in, or maybe try climbing up the side of the castle?"

I chuckled. "I didn't know you knew sarcasm."

Aislin lifted her chin, eyes blazing. "There's a lot you don't know about me."

Ouch. I straightened, bringing my extended hand to my heart. "You wound me, princess. I may not know everything about you, but I'm willing to learn—if you are." She ducked her head, cheeks flushing a bright red. "And climbing the wall isn't a bad idea—if we had the right equipment."

I couldn't help smirking. Pale, beautiful skin with a flash of color. What I wouldn't do to see it again.

Someone cleared their throat. I shifted my gaze to Remy. He pushed up his glasses. I raised a brow.

"Are you two done?" He didn't wait for an answer. "Because if there is a patrol on the way then time is of the essence. Now then, I might have a temporary solution." Of course, he did. A wizard at its best.

"Okay, which is?" Aislin asked, brushing her hair off her shoulder.

The corners of Remy's lips lifted and spread open, revealing white teeth, which contrasted his dark skin.

"Invisibility."

Aislin's jaw dropped. Her eyes shifted my way then back to Remy. "Seriously?"

Remy nodded, his glasses falling down the bridge of his nose. "It's just a simple cloaking spell. But it only lasts a couple minutes."

I snorted. We were better off just waltz right in there than the stupid spell wearing off in the middle of sneaking.

Remy crossed his arms over his chest. "Do you have a problem with that, Elijah?"

My brows raised to the top of my forehead. "Me?" I glanced around, pressing a hand to my chest. "Me, have a problem with your idea? Oh, I don't know, maybe," I leaned forward, "I just think my plan is way better—at least we would know what we are getting ourselves into."

Remy frowned, brows furrowing. "I believe we already know what we are getting ourselves into—trouble." He turned to Aislin. "The invisibility spell may only last a short amount of time, but we may be able to sneak in and acquire some sort of uniform to blend as much as we can."

Aislin glanced at me, brows creased, and the corner of her lips turned up slightly. "It doesn't sound so bad."

I threw my hands up in the air and paced to the edge of the cliff. My jaw clenched. Didn't sound so bad. Ha. I ran a hand through my hair. My heart pumped hard and fast against my sternum. Don't think—do. That's what I do.

Why couldn't anyone understand that? My hands fell to my sides. I flexed them and tried to control the urge to shake both back to their senses. What would invisibility do for us? Nothing—just cause more havoc. I closed my eyes. Was I the one being irrational? My hand clenched, nails digging into my flesh. I wasn't a leader. I never made any decisions—so why start now?

I sighed and opened my eyes. Blue skies stared back— vast and unchanging, for now at least. Pain ripped through my chest and up my throat. I fell to one knee. My hand flew to my neck. I gasped for air, spots entering my vision.

"Elijah!" Aislin cried out. I couldn't reply.

Heat raced through my veins, the pain intensifying. My pulse thrashed in my ears. What was this . . . pain? Images flashed. Steel blue eyes and blood. Distant howls and the cloyingly sweet scent of fresh blood filled my senses. I crumbled further down and pressed my forehead against the cool earth. A fight to the death. I closed my eyes and let the visions play out.

A grey wolf circled me, hackles raised, and teeth bared. Saliva dripped from his jowls. Wolves of all shapes and sizes watched, claws flexing to join in. This was no normal fight. A snarl left my pulled back lips.

I followed his movements, muscles tensed. In a blink of an eye, he lunged. I jumped back. His teeth grazed my neck. Warmth trickled down. I licked my fangs and lunged forward. He met me in the middle. Teeth snapped, howls echoed in my ears, and a hollow crunch.

A whimper escaped then a gurgle. My body went limp.

I shook my head, scattering the images. My death. I swallowed the lump forming in my throat. A hand touched my back. Heat spread outwards. I tensed. Words filled my ears. *Kill Illium Dreamer and you will be free.* Free? My eyes snapped open. The pain slowly receded into a dull throb. I knew what needed to be done. I turned my head and met wide, blue eyes.

"Aislin." Her name rolled off my tongue like a wish.

She shivered, heart catching a beat. Her eyes searched mine. The corner of my lip lifted an inch.

"We need to go," she mumbled, glancing away. I nodded.

"The plan?" I asked, picking myself up. I swallowed, wincing slightly.

"The same thing it has been. Meet them head on. Sneaking will do us no good, you were right about that. However, I think invisibility could be used to our advantage, depending—that is—on how many guards are in the castle. If we can surprise a few and incapacitate them then we may stand a chance," Remy said, straightening his stance.

A grin spread across my lips. That's something I could do. My fingers itched for a fight.

"Sounds like a plan to me."

Aislin nodded, crossing her arms over her chest. "Fine. Let's do it then, before we lose the advantage."

I made the first move. Muscles taut as a string, I crept to the side of the castle. Stone grazed my shoulder as I kept as close as I could to the wall. Aislin's and Remy's footsteps followed close behind. My ears strained for any sound out of place. A catch of breath, a heavy placement of a foot, clinking metal. Crows cried and cawed, circling the spirals above. I paused, heart pounding in my ears.

No other movement. I pressed on. Maybe there wasn't anything to worry about. No guards, no danger. I frowned. A castle with no security was suspicious. My jaw clenched as I rounded the corner. The castle doors were shut with no guard in sight. No one watching the entrance meant only one thing—they knew we were here. Charging in was the only way. No point in disappointing him.

"The element of surprise might not be in our favor," I said, stopping for the moment to look at them.

"Shit," Remy cursed.

"We can still use the cloaking spell," Aislin said, "how long does it last for?"

Remy rubbed a hand down his face. "Ten minutes at the most, but I doubt it would last that long. I'd give it maybe five."

Aislin nibbled on her lower lip. My eyes travelled to her lips then her eyes then back again. Longing crashed into me. I wanted her lips on mine, to feel her quake in my arms, the slight catch of breath as she gave in. Her lashes fluttered, lips curving up. I gulped. When it was all over, I'd be free—free to be what I want.

Free to love with no worries, no strings attached. A soft breeze swirled by. Mahogany strands of hair whipped and lashed across her face. My heart stopped. Earth and rotten flesh drifted to my nose. Other scents filled my nostrils. Frigid air, and the sickly aroma of spoiled blood and dust.

Yup, no surprise attack.

"Be ready," I growled.

I wrinkled my nose and charged forward.

"Wait!" Remy called. I swiveled around and glared.

His Adam's apple bobbed as he swallowed. "The spell."

"I don't give a shit about the stupid spell. I can handle my own without it."

"We can't just waltz in there."
I smiled, eyes narrowing. "Watch me."

Chapter 26

Elijah

I didn't wait for a reply. There was no point. I knew what I was doing. Charging head first into danger was my nature. My hands pressed on the grey stone doors. A creak echoed— long and high-pitched. I winced. No turning back now.

Light filtered in from the outside, filling in the dark spaces. I blinked, my eyes adjusting to the drastic change. There he was. Illium. Tall and pale, a stark contrast to the dark hues around him. Violet eyes stared down at me then flickered passed me.

His eyes brightened. Frigid air rolled off his skin, dropping the temperature of the room a few degrees. I tensed. Two guards on either side stood at attention. Clothes of purple and blue covered their bodies. The colors of Illium's reign, I assumed.

The two on the left had the same white hair and indigo eyes as Illium. Elves. The other two were the spoiled blood and rotten flesh scents I had caught a whiff of. A vampire and a red cap. I grimaced. Both were bloodthirsty creatures.

"What a pleasant surprise, Aislin!" His eyes danced. "If I had known you were on the other side of that door, I'd have given you a more appropriate greeting."

Aislin pushed passed me to stand in front. Her hand rested on the hilt of her blade.

"What would you consider a suitable greeting, Illium? This seems fair enough to me."

A smirk spread across his pale lips. He raised his arms and spread them out. "This." Creatures of all kinds gathered into the hall. All wore the same colors of purple and blue. I wrinkled my nose. Too many smells.

I couldn't pinpoint any exact one. Ogres, gremlins, more vampires, more red caps, and one minotaur stood around him. Eyes of every shade imaginable from fiery red to milky white and the heady aroma of hormones filled my senses. A battle was imminent. No turning back now.

"You ready?" I whispered, catching Aislin's eye.

Her head bobbed up and down in slow motion. "As ready as I'll ever be."

"Aislin, the odds are not in our favor," Remy whispered back. He stood inches away from me.

Fear rolled off his skin. My jaw clenched. If they weren't ready to fight, then I'd do it for them. My hands flexed at my sides. This was it. Energy bubbled just under the surface. I licked my lips.

"Are you expecting something to happen?" I asked, locking eyes.

Illium's narrowed. "It is better to be prepared than unprepared, pup. One day you might learn that. I, however, assume there is a reason for your visit besides small talk."

I glanced at Aislin. Telling him would surely start war, but wasn't that what we wanted? Silence crept in like a predator stalking its prey. No one moved. The calm before the storm. Who would make the first move? Instinct held me back. I waited, calm and poised. When the time was right, I'd strike.

Out of the corner of my eye, Aislin shifted. Her body straightened: shoulders back and head held high. The corner of my mouth lifted slightly. No fear. If we were going down, we were going down swinging.

"I've heard rumors of a certain plan you have. I came to persuade you to change your mind, if these rumors are true." Illium's pale face lit up.

"Ah, I see!" He clapped his hands together. "Sadly, there is nothing you can say or do that would deter me from my objective."

Aislin nodded her head. "I was afraid of that. I have no other choice than to stop you."

Laughter filled the room, bouncing off the stone walls. I flinched—the noise unexpected to my ears.

Illium raised his arms further, encompassing all the creatures. "How, might I ask? There are only three of you. I have more than enough soldiers to destroy you, if I must."

Not if I could help it. There was no way I was going down that easily, and I had no doubt Aislin felt the same. My hands curled into fists. The creatures surrounding Illium shuffled and fidgeted. Restlessness settled in.

I skidded closer to Aislin. Honeysuckle drifted and swirled, filling my nostrils. I breathed it in. I leaned into her.

"Go for the head of the beast," I whispered.

She turned, a brow raised. "What?"

I shook my head. "You'll know what I mean when it's time, trust me."

She held my gaze a second longer before switching it back to Illium. *All right princess, show time.*

"Fine, then show me what you got, Illium."

His eyes turned lavender. A smirk plastered to his face. "Gladly." He brought his hands together.

All hell broke loose. War cries echoed off the walls. I scanned my surroundings for any familiar faces. Aislin and Remy disappeared in the throng of creatures. Damn it. Metal clashed against metal as warriors turned on each other. I could only assume it was Remy's doing, but I didn't have time to think too much on it as a red cap charged forward.

Beady black eyes and sharp teeth flew at me. I swatted it away, knocking it to the ground. I didn't have time to deal with this little pest. My eyes were set on a bigger target.

Black fur, blood red eyes, and two long horns protruding from his head. I locked onto the minotaur as it barreled into an elf.

My nails lengthened to claws as I strode through the crowd, swiping right then left, blood spilling with each contact. Creatures fell around my feet. Gurgles and sputters as death took them. I relished in it. The wolf howled for more.

A roar left my lips as I shoulder-tackled the minotaur. Chaos reigned around us. He stumbled backwards. Manure and earth clogged my nostrils, but I pushed on. The minotaur's breath fogged in front of his face. I wrinkled my nose.

He lowered his head. I tensed. The bull charged. I grinned and sidestepped inches away from being impaled. His horns instead found the red cap's torso as it flung itself at me again. Blood spewed and spurted from its lips. The heady aroma of the sickly-sweet drops and pools of blood played on my instincts. Saliva filled my mouth.

The wolf growled and clawed at my insides, wanting release. I pushed it down. The minotaur swung his head, flinging the corpse into the throng again. I squared my shoulders as he turned back to face me. He huffed out spittle and blood. Honeysuckle drifted on the frigid air. I lifted my head to the ceiling. She was close, but where? Movement caught in the corner of my eye.

Too late.

The bull raised his horns, catching my side, and roared. Air whooshed out of my lungs. Was this it? The way I died— again? I flailed, arms fluttering and grappling for any kind of purchase. My hands latched onto the horn stuck in my side.

I wrenched my body off it, pushing myself up higher. It sucked and slurped as the horn slid out. I shuddered. The bull whipped his head back and forth. His roar bounced off the walls. It rang in my ears as I held on for dear life. Warmth spread and trickled down my side.

Copper filled my mouth. God, I hoped Aislin was faring better than me. If she lived, I'd be happy. Sweat dribbled down my temples, pooling at the crook of my neck. Taking a deep breath, I launched myself off the bull's horn. He faltered. My back slammed into the stone floor. I gasped. Pain rippled through my body. My heart pounded in my ears, loud as a bass drum.

I clenched my hands, nails scraping against the stone. It was now or never. The wolf inside circled, snarling. If I let myself go, then I knew I could win, but what other price would I pay? I shook my head.

Don't think, do. I closed my eyes for a second and let loose. Pain ripped at my skin. Bones popped and snapped, reconfiguring to the form I desired. I shuddered. Where there was once skin was now long, brown fur.

I blinked. Colors faded. All that was left were the subtle scents of each creature and blood—so much blood. I licked my jowls, saliva frothing. The bull snorted and lowered his head again. My hackles rose, a snarl left my lips. He charged. I followed suit.

Blood splattered onto the floor. He roared. His triumph was cut short as my teeth snapped around the nape of his neck. My fangs dug into his thick flesh, ripping and tearing. His hands hooked around his back. Nails cut into my fur, finding the wound on my side. I yelped, but held firm.

His hands wrapped around me and yanked. I sailed through the air, but the damage was already done. The bull fell, unmoving. My body collided into a creature that smelled vaguely of the swamp. I stumbled back to my feet, panting.

Blood dripped from my jowls. I licked it away. Fists slammed into my back. Pain shot through my spine. A whimper escaped my throat. My eyelids fluttered. I crumbled to the ground.

"Elijah!" someone screamed. My ears perked, but I didn't move.

Screams splintered around me. The stone was cool against my cheek. Rest, that's what I needed. Just close my eyes for a second. The floor vibrated under my body. We were foolish. This was a suicide mission and we knew it. The scent of honeysuckle swirled and clung to my skin. Aislin. My eyelids lifted just enough to spot her inches away.

Mahogany hair swished as she moved. Her fingers gripped her bow staff. White energy pulsed on either end. Muscles taut, ready for the next attack. Blood spider-webbed down her right arm. She stabbed forward then swung it around. Her movements choreographed. A big blob of a creature stood still, blood dripping from the wounds. A beefy hand grabbed the staff and pulled.

Aislin was off balance and fell headfirst. A fist connected with her cheek. I winced. She stumbled, but kept her grip on her staff. Aislin yanked it from the swamp thing, stepping back a bit. The creature flopped forward, swinging massive fists.

She blocked and dodged, her movements slightly sluggish. I licked the saliva from my lips and struggled to stand on all four wobbly legs. I snarled, steadying myself. Aislin turned, blue eyes finding mine. Fear rippled off her skin. I tilted my head to the right then back to the creature before us.

Her brow furrowed. I shook my head, spit flying, and charged the creature. She jumped back. I nipped at its ankles, forgetting for a moment about her. She was a distraction I didn't need. Fighting the urge to snap at her, I dug my fangs into the mud-covered flesh of the swamp thing. It howled, stomping its feet. I swiveled away, letting go for a second before going back to the same spot again. Blood coated my tongue.

It fell to one knee. Energy sizzled by my ear. Its head toppled, rolling a few inches away. My nostrils flared as I crept backwards. The battle raged on, but with less fever as before. My ears flattened against my scalp as I caught the eye of Illium. Ice clung to his pale skin. His face was a mask of fury. I shrunk back, growling. Metal scraped and clanked. A blade glinted in his hands, blood coating the tip. The chaos reached its climax, and we were at the center.

"Go for the head," Aislin whispered. "I understand now."

Her grip tightened on her staff as she flung herself back into the fray. I yelped and hobbled after her. More creatures fell around us. The warm liquid covered my paws, leaving a bloody path of paw prints.

We dodged and swiped, spun and jumped, until Illium was a foot away. Sweat and blood mingled on Aislin's exposed skin. Illium stalked toward us, his lips curving up.

My hackles rose. A growl emanated from my bared teeth.

"Illium."

His lips spread up further. "Aislin, I'm sad it has come to this, but I cannot let you leave here alive."

Her hands shook. "I was thinking the same thing."
He bowed. "So be it."

His blade flashed, lightning fast. It sliced into her arm. She sucked a breath, hissing through her teeth. I circled, ready to join if need be. Aislin swung down. He dodged. She lifted the other end at the same time. The blade cut into his underarm. He recoiled, his hand instantly cupping the wound. Blood dripped between his fingers.

Tension coiled like a snake ready to strike. Every noise and creature fell away around us, until it was just the battle before us. Illium and Aislin. A fight to the death. A soft voice screamed a name. A distraction. A single moment of slacked concentration was all it took. Aislin swiped to the right then up with the other end. Blood splattered from his lips.

One end of the blade protruded from his gut. His lifeforce ebbed and flowed. Illium's hands gripped the staff for a moment then let go. His hands fell to his sides. Silence filled the space where a battle once was.

"No!" The scream broke through the quiet. Feet moved and shuffled.

I closed my eyes, knowing who I would see. Vanilla drifted up my nostrils.

"I'm sorry, Kay," Aislin whispered, pain clear in her voice.

I opened my eyes and stared at the still form of Illium Dreamer, his body hunched over the blade. His pale skin even paler. White hair covered his face. Tears streaked down Aislin's cheeks. She didn't look my way, instead her eyes were glued to the form to my left. Kaydynce—the queen. I lowered my chin.

My ears flattened to either side of my scalp. There was no joy in this victory. There was a sucking sound as Aislin pulled out the blade. Illium's corpse toppled down, forehead resting on the stone floor.

Kaydynce rushed forward, pushing passed the onlookers, and curled his body into her lap. Blood coated her already red dress. She rocked his body back and forth, cradling it to her chest.

"This isn't happening. You can't die!" She tucked his head to her breast. "Don't leave me . . . please."

"I'm so sorry, Kaydynce. I wish there had been another."

"Get out!" Anger hissed and crackled in her hardened gaze. Aislin flinched, but turned to leave.

"Come on Elijah, let's find Remy." She walked off.

I nodded and turned to follow. A scent wafted in the air. I paused, ears straightening then flattening again. Worn leather and something else. I lifted my snout, hoping to catch the scent again. Tilting my head, I glanced at Kaydynce. A flicker of movement caught my eye. I froze. Golden eyes stared back at me, jaw falling open.

Mother fucker.

Chapter 27

Aislin

I'd killed him. My blade plunged into his stomach without a second thought. Illium Dreamer was dead . . . because of me. Kaydynce's scream echoed in my ears. The same horror and anguish I'd had when I'd watched Kaelin's lifeless body crumble to the ground. I did that. I was a killer, in every sense of the word.

I closed my eyes. Warm tears fell, but nothing could stop the pain or guilt that loomed around me. There was nothing I could do. Was there another way? Didn't matter, anymore.

"Remy?" I called, unsure if I would hear a reply.

"Oh, thank God you're alive, Aislin," he said, stumbling toward me.

I let out the breath I was holding. I was, but Illium wasn't. "Me too," I mumbled, studying him.

Cuts and slashes covered his bare skin, but there were no other obvious wounds. Remy pushed up his glasses. One of the lenses was cracked, creating a fractured mirror image of his brown eyes.

"Where's Elijah?" he asked, looking around.

I frowned and glanced behind me. "I thought he was behind me." A tuft of brown fur caught my eye. "Oh, there he is."

Elijah trotted forward, tongue lolling. I rested a hand on his head. "Let's get the hell out of here."

Remy nodded. "Indeed." He raised his hands and mumbled gibberish.

A doorway appeared, glowing a bright white.
"Aislin!"

We all turned in time to see Kaydynce marching toward us with what was left of Illium's army. Three elves, two red caps, and four vampires. Damn, we'd done a number on them.

"I'll never forgive you for this!"

I closed my eyes. I wouldn't either. The price was too high, yet I'd done it anyways. "I don't blame you, Kaydynce."

Tears streamed down her pink cheeks. Sapphire eyes dimmed. "He was all I had. Now I have nothing. I hope you're happy."

I turned away. Happiness was a luxury I couldn't afford anymore. I strode through the doorway and never looked back. The minute my feet touched the studio floor, I crumbled. Pain ripped at my heart. Dull throbs entered next, reminding me of every hit I'd received. I welcomed it. Focusing on the physical pain was better than the emotion.

A hand rested on my shoulder. Warmth spread through my arm. I lifted my eyes to meet Remy's.

"You did what you had to. Not all decisions are easy." I nodded, sniffling. "I know. I just . . . I killed him, Remy.

How am I supposed to live with myself?"

The corner of his lip turned up. "Like everyone else— learn from it, then move on."

"Easier said than done," I grumbled.

Remy chuckled, his grip tightening on my shoulder. "Most things are."

Learn and move on. What could I possibly learn from it? That death is senseless? That everyone dies?

"Um, guys?" I glanced at Elijah, in human form again, catching his hazel eyes. "I think I found something . . . or rather, someone."

My heart clenched, pulse speeding up. I gulped. Elijah fidgeted and looked away, avoiding my gaze. Silence followed his words. Who did he find? Could it be . . . but how?

He sucked in a breath then let it out slowly, raising sad eyes. I raised my brow. Was this supposed to be suspenseful?

Time ticked by—second by second.

"Who?" I asked, patience running thin.

Elijah's lips tightened into a straight line. "Kaelin. I know where he is."

My heart stopped. My breath caught in my throat. I swallowed. "Where?" I wheezed.

His brows furrowed, lips pursing. "The Reaper's Realm."

www.ingramcontent.com/pod-product-compliance
Lightning Source LLC
Chambersburg PA
CBHW061435150726
47987CB00001B/225